Dream y...
Pursue ...
hive your ...
They do come true.
Mine did!
Daniel

blood of the
DONNELLYS

Daniel L. McRae
2012

blood of the DONNELLYS

David McRae

A SANDCASTLE BOOK

A MEMBER OF THE DUNDURN GROUP
TORONTO

Editor: Michael Carroll
Design: Erin Mallory
Printer: Webcom

Library and Archives Canada Cataloguing in Publication

McRae, David, 1948-
    Blood of the Donnellys / David McRae.

ISBN 978-1-55002-754-9

    I. Title.

PS8625.R33B56 2008   jC813'.6   C2007-905731-4

1 2 3 4 5   12 11 10 09 08

Conseil des Arts du Canada   Canada Council for the Arts

ONTARIO ARTS COUNCIL
CONSEIL DES ARTS DE L'ONTARIO

Canada

We acknowledge the support of **The Canada Council for the Arts** and the **Ontario Arts Council** for our publishing program. We also acknowledge the financial support of the **Government of Canada** through the **Book Publishing Industry Development Program** and **The Association for the Export of Canadian Books**, and the **Government of Ontario** through the **Ontario Book Publishers Tax Credit** program, and the **Ontario Media Development Corporation**.

Care has been taken to trace the ownership of copyright material used in this book. The author and the publisher welcome any information enabling them to rectify any references or credits in subsequent editions.

J. Kirk Howard, President

Printed and bound in Canada.
www.dundurn.com

Dundurn Press
3 Church Street, Suite 500
Toronto, Ontario, Canada
M5E 1M2

Gazelle Book Services Limited
White Cross Mills
High Town, Lancaster, England
LA1 4XS

Dundurn Press
2250 Military Road
Tonawanda, NY
U.S.A. 14150

For my parents

Acknowledgements

My earliest memories of the Donnelly family came from my mother's and father's stories. From the late 1940s to the mid-1960s, our family lived in Clinton, Ontario. We made regular shopping excursions to London, Ontario, along Highway 4 through Lucan. It is in Lucan that the stories would begin. We made several side trips to view the Donnelly tombstone (the original) at St. Patrick's Roman Catholic Church and took short drives up the Roman Line to locate the Donnelly farm.

I revisited the Donnelly Homestead in July 2000. I spent a very pleasant summer afternoon with J. Robert Salts, the current owner, as he recounted his experiences living at the Donnelly Homestead, which are vividly described in his book *You Are Never Alone: Our Life on the Donnelly Homestead*. I wish to thank Mr. Salts for his encouraging words of success on the publication of my novel and for his permission to use his name and the Donnelly Homestead in my story.

It is important that the history of the Donnelly family be told and told again. It is through these varied tellings that, hopefully, the tragic consequences of modern-day violent acts of prejudice and bullying afflicting many of our people today, young and old, may be addressed.

Chapter 1

Squirming at the defence lawyer's table in the Toronto courthouse, I wiped sweaty palms on my grey dress pants and ran a finger under the starched collar of my white shirt. I wanted desperately to loosen the knot of my red tie and shed the blue blazer I was wearing. Mom had bought these clothes for my trial. Our lawyer had insisted I be well dressed to make a good impression for my courtroom appearance. I faced a charge of committing damage to public property over one thousand dollars.

"It'll be over soon, Jason. Be brave!"

I turned around and nodded at Jennifer's warm smile. Jennifer was my twin sister. Her freckled face and auburn hair matched my own. We both carried our tall fifteen-year-old frames with good posture. Jennifer had supported me through all my bad times, yet I now remembered our last fight, one of too many in the past few months.

"Stay away from them, Jason!" Jennifer warned me. "They're jerks!"

"What do you know, Stilts?" I sneered. "I choose my own friends!"

Jennifer's face grew red at the nickname that teased her about her height. "I … I know you skipped school four times in the past month. I know you've been hanging around the mall with Derek and Kirk. *They're too old for you and they deal drugs."*

"Says who? Besides, I'm fifteen and they're only seventeen. What's two years?"

As I slammed my bedroom door, shutting her out, I felt a twinge of guilt when I saw the wounded look on her face.

Not long after that the police arrived at our front door to talk to my parents and me about the shoplifting at Zellers. The officers laid no charges. They had no real proof. The police found none of the stolen CDs in my backpack or anywhere in our house, but one witness insisted she saw me lift the discs and tuck them into a side pocket of the pack. She was right. I did steal the discs, but I'd slipped the stolen property to Derek and Kirk, who escaped through the mall's underground parking lot. Nevertheless, my parents grounded me. Despite my harsh words to Jennifer, though, she never once criticized me and gave me the benefit of the doubt about my innocence.

Now, in the courtroom, I glanced quickly at my sister again, then at my parents. *How did I get here?* I stared at the judge's empty podium. It and the room's tables and chairs gleamed with a golden oak finish. The walls were off-white from the ceiling to midpoint where oak wainscoting completed the decoration. A heavy blue carpet covered the floor, and tall arched windows lined the street wall. The windows revealed the glowering grey skies, slushy streets, and dirty snowbanks of late January. The dreary outside winter weather did nothing to warm the stark setting of the courtroom.

"When is that judge going to get here?" I asked my lawyer, who was sitting beside me.

Mr. Roberts squeezed my arm gently. "Not long now. You've done the right thing, son."

I sighed. Everything that had happened over the past several months seemed a blur. My failing report card from first-term Grade 10, my absences from high school, the shoplifting incident at Zellers — they were all jumbled together. Then there was the business at Becker's ...

"How's it going, Jas?" Kirk asked, a sneer on his face. Both he and Derek were slouched against the big maple tree outside our school on a blustery October afternoon. "We gotta job and we need you!"

"No way!" I protested. "The heat was really on me after Zellers, and things are finally starting to cool down."

Derek leered as he pushed his chest into mine and leaned closer. "But they could get warmer. One quick call to the right people and you're toast, my friend!"

I hated the deep-throated chuckle Derek used when he had control of someone.

"You wouldn't dare!" I gasped.

"Don't bet on it," Derek said menacingly, his cold blue eyes drilling into my own.

I flinched, then dropped my gaze to the ground. "W-what have you got in mind?"

"That's better!" Kirk said, grinning at my surrender to Derek's threat. "The pop machine at Becker's is an easy touch. You'll see."

I agreed to meet Derek and Kirk at the local variety store in the late evening after it closed. When I got there at midnight, the lights in the place were off. I took up sentry alongside the pop machine not far from the front door, nervously watching for my mother to drive by on her return from a night shift at the hospital. It was past my curfew. If she spotted me, I'd really be in trouble. Shivering, I retreated into the shadows.

A few minutes later a sports utility vehicle screeched to a stop in front of the Becker's. Derek emerged from the driver's side, and Kirk got out of the front passenger seat. Both headed immediately for the pop machine.

"What are you doing?" I whispered hoarsely at them. Both teens were carrying crowbars.

Kirk tossed me a third bar as they reached me, then they started prying the lock on the machine's door, while I stood awkwardly to one side.

"If you're not going to help us, stupid, keep watch!" Derek growled as he heaved his weight on the bar against the door. The shattering plastic and the grinding metal made a lot of racket. Then, just as the lock snapped, all three of us heard something moving inside the store.

A man rushed out, waving his arms. "Hey, you punks! Stop!"

Kirk, Derek, and I froze. Who was this? The store's manager and clerk should have been long gone.

Before I could react, the charging man collided with me on the sidewalk in front of the pop machine. Derek and Kirk had bolted to the SUV and were already roaring down a side alley. The man gripped me by the shirt collar and hauled me into the store. The police arrived minutes later. The man who had grabbed me was the owner of the store. He had been doing some late-night inventory work. I had been caught red-handed.

The police handcuffed me and took me to the police station for questioning. After a phone call home, my parents arrived at the station with Mr. Roberts, the family lawyer. After several hours of questioning, the police released me, as a young offender, to the custody of my parents. As we left the station, Derek and Kirk stepped out of another squad car. I stopped and watched the two shuffle toward me.

As we passed one another, Kirk growled under his breath, "Keep your mouth shut, punk!"

Later I learned that the police had stopped Derek for speeding at a hundred kilometres an hour in a sixty-kilometre zone. The police had recognized the two teens from the descriptions radioed to them. Their SUV belonged to Derek's dad, who had reported it stolen earlier that afternoon. Upon searching the trunk, the police had discovered two small packs of marijuana.

Then came the last of a series of meetings with Mr. Roberts. My parents and Jennifer had accompanied me. "Jason!" the lawyer cautioned. "You've been identified at the scene. If you cooperate with the police and the Crown attorney, you'll get a maximum of thirty hours of community service with no criminal record, especially since you're not involved in the drugs."

At first I stubbornly refused. "Not a chance!" I told him. "I won't rat on my friends."

"Jason, please!" Jennifer cried.

"Mind your own business, Stilts!" I snapped.

I even shut out the sobs of my mother. "They know me, Mom." I told her. "They'll find me."

"No, Jason," my father said, "they won't." He stood before me, staring deeply into my eyes. I had never seen such a concentrated look from him before. "Listen to Mr. Roberts. It's the only chance you have."

Finally, I agreed to testify through a closed-circuit television that fed into the courtroom. Kirk and Derek received sentences of thirty hours of community service and twelve months' probation for possession of marijuana, with an additional twenty hours of community service and fifteen months' probation for attempted robbery. They began serving their sentences concurrently. Derek's dad dropped the charges on the stolen SUV.

Focusing again on the vacant podium in the courtroom, I cursed the tardiness of the judge, then risked another brief look over my shoulder. I wished I hadn't. Dad was staring at the high ceiling. His gaunt face seemed even more drawn than usual. The hollow sockets around his eyes were deeper, and the black rings were darker. His immaculate black hair normally shone. Now I noticed a cowlick at the back of his head, and his hair was uncombed. His blue pinstriped suit, though neatly pressed, hung loosely over his thinning frame.

Mom was slumped in the bench seat and was shakily removing her tinted glasses. As she fidgeted with her dangling auburn curls, I gasped at the redness encircling her eyes. Quickly, I blinked back tears.

"All rise!"

I jumped at the echoing command from the court clerk. Everyone stood. Mr. Roberts and the Crown attorney bowed to recognize the judge's entrance. A short, stout man in a long, flowing black robe with a red shoulder sash climbed the few short steps to the judge's bench. We all remained standing until the judge seated himself in a high-backed leather chair. The judge opened a thin brown file folder, adjusted his half-rimmed glasses on the bridge of his nose, and studied the case documents.

"Jason Stevens!" he barked.

Mr. Roberts nudged me, and we both got to our feet and faced the judge.

"Mr. Stevens, you've been charged with mischief to private property over a thousand dollars. You've entered a plea of guilty, which has been confirmed by your own lawyer and accepted by the Crown attorney. Is that your wish?"

"Yes, Your Honour."

"As you have no prior records and you've cooperated with the Crown's office to bring this incident to a speedy close, I accept the plea of mercy from Mr. Roberts, your lawyer. You are hereby sentenced to thirty hours of community service in Toronto to begin immediately. Do you wish to address the court?"

I glanced at Mr. Roberts. "Your Honour," the lawyer said, "the Stevens family is taking up residence in the village of Lucan near London at the beginning of February. That's just a few days from now. I respectfully request that Jason be allowed to begin his sentence after his family has arrived in Lucan and settled in their new home."

The judged peered over his tilted glasses as Mr. Roberts continued. "Prior arrangements have been made for Jason to assist his grandfather in a community history project to update the archives at the new museum wing being set up in Lucan. He'll also be involved in community research and service for senior citizens at the Lucan nursing home."

I looked sharply at Mr. Roberts and then at Dad, who returned my gaze and nodded briefly to let me know the decision was final.

"Your request is granted!" the judge said. "Court adjourned!"

Mom cried softly as Jennifer dashed through the swinging gate that separated the spectators' seating from the court area and threw her arms around my neck. I returned the warm hug. Mom soon joined us, and we stood in a group clinch for several minutes.

I watched Dad over Mom's shoulder. Slowly, he rose from his seat. He seemed older to me — more stooped and paler than before. I clutched Mom and Jennifer more tightly as Dad moved toward us. I waited. Dad touched my shoulder and smiled. I recognized the familiar glint in his eyes. He was a caring man, and I knew he'd forgiven me.

The pangs of guilt started almost immediately as Dad led us to the back of the courthouse. They increased as we stepped into the freezing wind whipping around the parking lot. Even the warmth of a heated car and my family's forgiveness didn't diminish the sinking feeling in the pit of my stomach. How would I ever repay my family for its love and support? The task seemed impossible. I didn't know where to turn for advice or comfort. My guilt had even pushed Jennifer away.

The family sat silently in the car as we drove home for one of the last times. As Mr. Roberts had said, we planned to leave in a couple of days for Lucan. Dad was taking a job as a freelance writer and photographer with the local Lucan newspaper. Mom began her new nursing job in nearby London soon, too.

Mixed with the guilt was the resentment of the move. Jennifer and I had been born in Toronto and had lived our whole lives in the small two-storey three-bedroom house in suburban Etobicoke. Since the trial had begun, I'd had no time to really say goodbye to my friends, especially my best one, Sam.

To top it off, working with Granddad on a community history project appealed even less to me. I knew it would only be three or four hours on Saturdays after the museum closed, and that by March break my sentence would end, but Granddad, a retired history teacher from the local high school, was rather eccentric.

On previous visits I'd noticed that people politely smiled with what appeared to be pity upon greeting Granddad. I saw, too, that they shrugged and shook their heads as they passed by. I loved Granddad dearly, but his research project on the Donnellys, an Irish-Canadian family that had been slaughtered by a vigilante mob more than a hundred years ago, and the ghostly sightings at their former homestead, only made people see him as a kook even more. On some occasions, unknown to Mom and Dad, teenagers teased Granddad in downtown Lucan. Nothing serious enough to call the police, but enough to make me angry and embarrassed.

Granddad always laughed them off, simply saying, "Kids will be kids!"

As soon as Dad turned into our driveway and shut off the engine, I pushed open the rear passenger door and stalked into the house. Jennifer tried to catch me as I fumbled with the key in the lock, but I broke away from her, went inside, scrambled up the stairs, and slammed my bedroom door. Turning on my stereo, I parted the curtains to look at my family, who were still outside. I never wanted to hurt anyone — especially Jennifer — but that's exactly what I did every time.

My sister was wiping away tears as she leaned against Mom's shoulder. When my stereo erupted in an echoing thud of heavy metal music, Jennifer glanced up at my window. Quickly, I jerked the curtains closed.

"Let him be for now!" I heard my dad say as he tried to soothe Jennifer. "He'll be fine in a day or two. You'll see!"

Chapter 2

A couple of days later I awoke with a terrific headache. Opening one eye, I glanced at my bedside radio clock — 7:30 a.m.! I sat up. How could that be? Hadn't I just gone to sleep? Rubbing sleep from my eyes, I heard a relentless pounding that wasn't in my head.

"Jason!" I recognized Jennifer's voice. "Get up! Dad wants to take us out for breakfast before the movers get here."

"Go away!"

It was moving day. We really were going to Lucan. Anger flooded through me again. I knew I'd been particularly mean to Jennifer and unfair to my parents the past few days, but it was my life, too. What right did they have to take me away from my home and friends just because they thought it would be good for me?

"Come on!" she pleaded. "Mom and Dad are waiting."

"Tell them no thanks!" I snarled. "I'm going to stay behind."

"Jason!"

"Get lost, Stilts!"

I threw my pillow at the opening door. In my sleepy stupor I missed and knocked the lamp off the bookcase, which grazed Jennifer's shoulder as it crashed to the floor. I froze under Jennifer's stare. What was I doing?

Jennifer and I could always talk in the past. Now I tried to speak, explain things, but my jaw just flapped. I got off my bed and reached out to Jennifer as tears welled in her eyes, but she turned away and slammed the door behind her.

Slumping back onto the bed, I started punching the other pillow. I hit it even harder when I heard Dad ask in the hallway, "Jennifer, where's Jason?"

"He's not coming!" Jennifer said, seething.

"Not coming? We'll see about that. Jason, get down here!"

I wrapped the pillow around my ears and covered my head with the blanket as I waited for him to burst into the room. I really couldn't blame him for being angry, but I didn't care. Instead I steeled myself for another fight with him.

"Wait, Tom!" I heard my mother say. "Let him be. He needs time."

"But, Ellen!" Then he sighed. "Come on, Jennifer, get your coat. I'm buying breakfast."

When I heard the front door close, I slipped off my bed, went over to the window, and looked out. Mom and Jennifer were walking arm in arm ahead of Dad. Jennifer rested her head on my mother's shoulder, a burst of frosty breath shrouding her. Dad tightened the scarf around his neck and buttoned his overcoat. Before climbing into the car, he glanced up at my window. At first he seemed dejected — not angry or disappointed, just sad. Then, slowly, he raised a hand in a gentle wave and smiled. After that he got into the car, started it, and reversed down the driveway. In a few moments the car disappeared in the morning fog.

"Why do they have to be so nice?" I muttered.

After flipping on the stereo to my usual brand of heavy metal, I flopped face first into a pillow and closed my eyes.

As I lay there and let myself be enveloped by the electric skirl of guitars, I barely heard my cell phone ring. Fumbling for the phone, I picked it up, punched the talk button, and mumbled, "Hello?"

"Hey, man!" I knew Sam's voice right away and turned down the volume on my stereo. "You must be having some kind of blast there, kiddo! What's up?"

"You know what's up!" I shot back. "I move today. Remember?"

"Yeah ... I know."

Sam resented the move as much as I did, if not more. I smacked my hand across my forehead, regretful that I was even being snarly with my best friend. "Sorry for snapping, Sam!" I struggled to keep the quaver out of my voice. "It's just that ...

"Tough, isn't it? I'm coming over. See you in a bit."

"Thanks, man."

I tossed the cell onto the bed, got up, and threw on jeans and a Toronto Maple Leafs T-shirt. Then, from outside, I heard the rumble of a big engine and the bleeping whine of a reverse signal. The moving truck was backing into our driveway. I wanted to shout, "Go away! Leave us alone!" Instead I turned up my stereo to block out the noise of the movers.

"Anyone home?" a voice called out.

I pushed myself out of bed, trudged out of the room, and looked over the banister of the upstairs landing. A burly man was standing in the foyer. He tilted his sweat-rimmed baseball cap on his head and quickly surveyed the hall, then took some measurements of the front door and tapped out the hinge pins to move it out of the way. As he straightened, he spotted me. "Hey, Jason! It's Fred! The door was open. I know we're a bit early, but I thought we might as well get started."

I didn't answer. We'd met the first time he'd come to give an estimate on our move, and he'd seemed friendly enough then. Now I was in no mood for chatter.

"Mom and Dad not home?" he asked.

"Gone out for breakfast," I grumbled. "Be back whenever!" His smile faded.

"It is okay if we start, isn't it?"

"Whatever!"

I returned to my bedroom and shut the door. When I heard the rattle of the moving truck's back door and then the crash of the loading ramp on our front steps, it just made my mood blacker. With all the noise from the shuffle of furniture, the barking of orders, and my blasting stereo, I didn't hear the tap on my bedroom door at first. When the knocking became louder, I flew off the bed.

"What do you want now?" I bellowed.

The door suddenly opened and knocked me two steps backward. It was Sam! As always, his freckled, chubby face wore a grin.

"Easy, buddy!" he said, ducking behind the door for protection when he saw my scowl.

I relaxed. "Sorry. Come in."

Sam shut the door and checked the candy bowl on the bureau, but it was empty today. He threw himself on my bed. "Boy, did you see the arms on those movers? They've got muscles on their muscles and arms as big as my legs."

I shrugged. "Life sucks!"

Sam flashed another grin. "It won't be that bad, Jase. It's not like you'll be a million miles away. We both have cells. Besides, I'll be paying you a visit during March break."

I frowned but didn't say anything.

Sam riffled through a copy of *Sports Illustrated*. After a few minutes, he asked, "What did the judge say you have to do again?"

"I have to do thirty hours of community service helping Granddad in Lucan."

Sam chuckled. "Your grandfather! What a guy! What he's up to these days?"

"See!" I snapped. "You're just like everybody else! Making fun of him all the time. And now I have to hang around him. I'm sure glad no one knows me in Lucan."

"Whoa, Jase! Your granddad's a great guy. Sure, he may seem weird to some people, but I think he's always doing neat things. I was just asking what he's doing lately. You don't have to bite my head off."

"I'm sorry, Sam. I'm just on edge these days. Granddad's doing a history of Lucan and helping set up the village's new museum wing."

"Is that all you have to do? Work in a museum and help your granddad with local history? What's the big deal?"

"And help out with senior citizens."

Sam snorted. "Poor guy! That's some serious hard time."

"You don't get it," I growled. "He's digging up more stuff about the Donnellys."

"You mean the Black Donnellys? From what your folks have told me, and what we've read in school, people in Lucan aren't going to like that very much."

"Exactly," I said. "Some of the villagers rarely speak to him anymore. Even his oldest friends have warned him off."

"Geez! He's really into it, isn't he? But your granddad never lets other people's opinions stop him. You know that."

"Yeah, but …" I held my breath for a moment to stifle my anger. "Now he's studying trance clairvoyance."

Sam sat upright. "Say what?"

"Ghosts! He's studying ghosts! The other kids in town have a hoot wisecracking about him. And I have to move there to work with him. Lucky me, eh?"

"But where are the ghosts in Lucan?"

"Out on the old Donnelly Homestead on the Roman Line. Granddad's made friends with a Mr. Salts, the current owner of the old Donnelly farm. He's another ghostbuster!"

Sam whistled. "Cool!"

"Sam! Not you, too." I knew Sam secretly enjoyed many of my grandfather's antics. Given the chance, I think he would have loved to work with him.

"Come on, Jase! You've read William Bell's *Five Days of the Ghost* and thought it was pretty cool, too."

"Yeah, I know."

"We even did some research into ghosts and hauntings for our project on the book! You really got off on the whole theory of the etheric body, the half-stage between physical and spiritual bodies after death."

He was right. I did enjoy that project.

Sam jumped on my silence. "Give your granddad a chance. He's an okay guy."

Just then I heard laughter float up from the front foyer.

"Jason, we're home!"

I recognized my mother's voice, then heard quick steps come up the stairs and stop at my door. A gentle tap followed.

"Jason? Can I come in?"

Sam slapped my arm and nodded at the door. "She's my friend, too. I also came to say goodbye to Jennifer."

Slowly, I got up and opened the door. "Hi, Jen," I said sheepishly. "How was breakfast?"

I melted at the sight of my sister's warm smile and stepped back to let her into my room. Jennifer reached out and placed a hand on my shoulder. I didn't draw back this time.

"It was great," she said. "But I missed you."

I nodded and let my head droop.

"Sam!" She raced over to the bed and bounced beside him.

I watched and listened as the two bantered. After dodging a pillow thrown by Sam, I joined in the laughter and retelling of old memories. Then, as they continued gabbing, I tried to finish up the last of my packing, wrestling the bedding off the bed they still occupied.

"Jennifer! Jason!" Mom called from downstairs.

"Coming, Mom!" Jennifer piped up.

I had mellowed with Sam's visit, but I wasn't as ready yet as Jennifer to accept this new start in our lives. When I pushed the top drawer of my bureau a little too hard, my baseball trophies fell over.

"Your father wants to get going," Mom said. She was now in the hallway and was peering into my room. "Jason, the movers are going to do your room shortly. It looks like you still have a few things to pack, though."

"I'm almost done," I said. "Sam's here. Jen and I are just saying goodbye."

Mom smiled. "Hello, Sam." She backed out of the room. "Don't be too long, okay?"

The three of us sat in silence. It was hard for me to keep back the tears. I blinked rapidly as I shook my best friend's hand. Jennifer openly let the tears flow and hugged Sam a little tighter and a little longer than usual.

"See you later, Freckle Face," she whispered to Sam.

"Not if I see you first!" Sam said, his voice quavering uncertainly.

We all shuffled down the stairs and quietly shrugged into our heavy winter coats. Mom and I looked at each other. I smiled, and she put her arms around my shoulders so as not to embarrass me completely in front of Sam.

"We're off, Fred!" I heard Dad say from the kitchen. "We'll see you in Lucan."

"Right you are, Mr. Stevens. Safe journey!"

Dad held the front door open for us to leave. I let Mom and Jennifer go ahead. Dad followed Sam and me out but stepped around us to open the car.

"Take care, Sam!" I said.

We high-fived each other, and I scrambled into the empty back seat. Jennifer and I waved at Sam, who lingered on our front steps. Soon we were off in a cloud of exhaust and snow flurries. I settled back. My mellow mood had vanished and the anger was back.

Chapter 3

After we headed out of the Toronto area, drafts gusted in between the door jambs and window frames of our car. Jennifer threw me a warm comforter. I gathered the blanket around me, smiled a thank-you to Jennifer, closed my eyes, and fell asleep. The gentle rocking of the car in the snow squall helped to lull me, but I still heard snatches of conversation between my parents and Jennifer.

"Highway 23, next turn!" Dad said. "Used to be called Cedar Swamp Road a hundred years ago."

I felt the lurch of the car as it skidded in the rutted drifts lining the highway. The snow was falling more heavily now and the wind had increased steadily. I was too nervous to sleep anymore.

Jennifer poked me. "Welcome back, sleepyhead!" She was trying hard to cheer me up.

"Didn't miss much, did I?"

"Only about three accidents and an extra ten centimetres of snow!"

I sat up as the car skidded again. Wet snow built up on the wipers and the windshield with each passing swipe.

"Cedar Swamp School's next on our tour," Dad joked, trying to take our minds off the weather.

I groaned. He always had the same spiel whenever we came this way to Granddad's.

"School Section Number 4, built in 1874, and the meeting

place for the vigilantes who burned out the Donnellys."

I sighed and rolled my eyes. Still, Dad's history lesson did distract us from the storm.

"Today's February 4, isn't it?" Jennifer asked. "The anniversary of the Donnelly massacre?"

"You're right, Jennifer," Mom said. "You've heard this story before, haven't you, Jason?"

"Yeah, Mom, a million times."

I watched the blinding snowflakes hurtle toward us. The white wall of snow was hypnotizing me, so I was sure Dad was having a hard time keeping the car on the road.

"James Carroll, the constable from Lucan, led the vigilantes," Dad said. "They met at the schoolhouse early in the morning of the fourth. Between complaints about the Donnellys and several passes of the liquor jug, they decided the Donnellys had to go."

"But I've never understood why," I said, needing to keep my mind off the storm.

Mom and Dad looked at each other in surprise. Dad even glanced in his rearview mirror to make sure it was me in the back seat. After a short pause, he launched into the story again. "Jealousy, I gather."

"Jealousy?" Jennifer said. "I've never heard that before."

Nor had I. I leaned over Mom's seat to hear Dad better.

"The Irish," Dad continued, "were all hard workers, hard drinkers, and hard fighters. The Donnellys seemed better at all three than most. They farmed; they worked in logging camps and railway lines; they operated stagecoaches. They prospered in very hard times."

"But that doesn't seem to be enough reason to murder them." I was really awake now.

"It was a brutal life in Lucan in the mid-1800s," he

continued. "There were stories of farm thefts, livestock mutilations, fights, stagecoach feuds, and barn fires. Locals never forgave Jim Donnelly for the murder of Pat Farrell, even though he spent the seven years he was sentenced to in Kingston Penitentiary. While he was away, his wife, Johannah, raised their seven boys and daughter, Jennifer. The boys had to learn to take care of themselves and to look after their mother. They learned to work hard and defend themselves. Their reputations started early."

"But, Dad," Jennifer said, "that's still not enough reason to murder them."

"Tom!" Mom suddenly cried. "Look out!"

A flurry of blinding snow smothered the windshield as the car bucked a heavy snowdrift. I banged against Mom's seat and lurched toward Jennifer, grabbing her before she slammed her head into Dad's headrest. We both fell back against the bench seat.

"Thanks, Jason!" Jennifer whispered.

I grinned. "Watch it, Stilts!"

I knew she really hated that name, but this time I was using it to let her know we were still friends. She took the hint and smiled in return. Pushing myself closer to the window, I peered into the raging storm. Even though it was daytime, the sky shifted from light grey to a more ominous black.

"Jennifer," I said, "look at those strange clouds!"

She leaned across my chest and stared at the flowing shapes. "They look like galloping horses."

"Without heads," Dad said. "Legend, rumour if you will, has it that you can see galloping headless horses in the night sky over the Roman Line every February 4."

"Wow!" Jennifer and I said at the same time.

As I studied the ghostly clouds drifting across the bleak sky, one of the blackest shapes veered across the hood of the car and momentarily blocked Dad's view of the road. As the vehicle bounced in the snowdrifts and spun in a full circle, the countryside flashed before our eyes and we hurtled helplessly across the road into the ditch on the opposite side. When the car hit the ditch, a wall of snow covered the back window. Dazed and confused, we all started to talk and move at once.

"Sit still!" Dad ordered. He seldom raised his voice, and when he did, he always got everyone's attention. Slowly, he opened his door and stepped into a knee-deep drift. "We're stuck!"

"Stuck! But, Tom —" Mom said, beginning to panic.

"Easy, Ellen," Dad soothed. "We turned on the Roman Line about two kilometres back. My dad's place isn't far. See! There's Rob Salts's place, the old Donnelly Homestead. We're nearly there."

"What was that shadow?" Jennifer asked, shivering. She had moved from her rear seat.

Dad chuckled. "The Midnight Lady, I imagine."

"Who?" I gasped.

"Thomas Kelley's Midnight Lady. According to him, she rides every February 4 on the Roman Line, seeking revenge for the Donnellys."

"Really?" I'd heard more stories about the Donnellys in one day than ever before in my life, even from Granddad.

"Let's go, Jason!" Dad said. "We'll walk to Granddad's and get his tractor to pull us out. Ellen and Jennifer, you stay here."

"But, Tom!" Mom protested.

"It'll be better for you and Jennifer to wait in the car and keep warm," Dad said. "We'll be back in a jiffy. I promise."

Dad and I began walking. Smooth, wind-sculpted snowbanks stretched everywhere I looked. Some tapered into the surrounding open spaces, while others filled the road's width.

"Dad," I said after we'd struggled about halfway to Granddad's, "do you believe those stories you told me?"

"What stories?" he said as he laboured awkwardly through the snow.

I knew he had other things on his mind, but I wanted an answer. Besides, I figured talking about the Donnellys might help us keep our minds off the storm. "Those ghost stories about — never mind."

Dad turned and faced me, blinking away some swirling snowflakes. "No, I don't really believe in ghosts. I've heard those stories ever since I was your age. Most people around here don't like to talk about the Donnellys at all. Those that do seem to add to the tales with each telling. Even Rob Salts doesn't put too much faith in some of the stories he hears."

"But I thought he was a trance clair ..."

"Clairvoyant," Dad finished. "That's right. He's a professional and has studied the issues extensively. But at the same time he's quite serious about the history of the Donnelly family and won't accept anything but the facts. He offers a great tour of his farm. We should go someday this spring."

Plodding headfirst into the storm, we nearly missed Granddad's lane. The snow was piled almost as high as the posts marking his laneway. We climbed over the drifts on our hands and knees until we reached my grandparents' back door. Dad pounded heavily — Granddad was slightly deaf and his eyesight was blurred. After about the fifth bang, we heard footsteps shuffling across the kitchen floor. A loud crash erupted, and Granddad muttered a curse. Soon the flowered lace curtains parted from the window on the back door.

"Who's there?" Granddad demanded.

"Dad, it's Jason and me! Open up!"

"I'm not opening to anybody! Not on a day like this!"

We both heard a metallic click.

"Back off and go away!" Granddad barked, pointing his shotgun through the window.

"For heaven's sake!" A small grey head with a round hair bun at the back peeked over the windowsill. "Put that gun down, you old fool!"

I laughed. Grandma might be tiny, but she sure could make Granddad obey.

"But, Mother!" he protested.

"Mom!" Dad called. "Let us in!"

Grandma glanced through the frosted window, and her eyes bulged. "It's Tom!" she cried. "And Jason's with him. Open the door for them."

"Tom?" he huffed. "Why didn't you say so in the first place?"

The door jerked open, and we both stumbled in. Grandma hugged me and shook the snow off Dad's neck and shoulders. After hanging our coats on the rack near the wood-burning stove, she hurried to plug in the electric kettle.

"Not now, Mom!" Dad said. "Ellen and Jennifer are stuck in the drift at the end of the line. Tom and I will just get warm and dry out a bit. Dad, can we borrow your tractor?"

Granddad didn't answer. Instead he buried himself in the utility closet and muttered a soft curse as his shotgun thudded on the floor. Finally, he emerged with his eyeglasses skewed crookedly over his face, grey tufts of hair spread in every direction, and his scarf drooped around his neck. "Give me a minute to fire the tractor up!" he told us as he tugged on his knee-high winter field boots.

I looked at my dad, who smiled, shook his head, and raised both eyebrows.

"We'll be back, Mother!" Granddad said. "Keep the kettle warm. Let's go, Tom! You, too, Jason!"

Dad and I put our coats back on and tumbled down the back stoop and out to the barn. "He sure doesn't change, does he?" I said to Dad, and we both grinned.

"Wait there!" Granddad ordered. He trudged through the snow blocking the lane to the barn. Dad and I started to follow him when we saw him struggle with the barn door, which was stuck in the snowdrifts. "Stay there!" he commanded, shoving one last time. The door skittered along its roller track, and Granddad toppled through the door but quickly staggered to his feet.

"Granddad!" I called. "Are you all right?"

I relaxed when I heard a string of swear words and saw him angrily brush the snow from his coat collar. Then he climbed onto the tractor, a 1948 Massey-Ferguson, and pulled the choke out to three-quarters full — no more or it would flood, he'd always warn. Next he twisted the key to the on position and pressed the starter. The engine coughed, and a black puff of smoke belched from the exhaust pipe. Then nothing more.

"Come on, old girl!" he coaxed. "Just one more time!"

Again he stamped on the starter button. This time the engine caught and the whole tractor shuddered. He dropped the gear into reverse, and the old tractor lurched out the door, easily cutting through the snow.

"Hop on, boys!" he cackled as he stopped beside us.

Dad and I each grabbed a rear fender and balanced on the hitch tongue. Pushing the choke all the way in and opening the throttle full speed, Granddad headed down the lane to the Roman Line. I had enjoyed rides with Granddad on the back of his tractor since I was barely old enough to crawl onto it. Smelling the musty farm odours and the stale, sweet scent of pipe tobacco that lingered in the folds of his winter coat, I smiled, then chuckled to myself when I sniffed a faint whiff of brandy. Granddad always kept a small "medicine" flask inside his inner coat pocket.

In no time at all Granddad was hooking his drag chain to the front bumper of our car and easing the vehicle out, which was empty. Apparently, Jennifer and Mom had left a note saying they'd gone to Mr. Salts's farm. I helped Dad clear the snow-crusted windows and check all the doors to make sure none had sprung during the accident.

Satisfied that everything was in good shape, Dad jumped into the driver's side and turned the ignition. The engine started on the first try. Rolling down the window, he said, "Jason, stay with Granddad and help him gather his chains. I'm going to get your mother and Jennifer."

"Nice folks, those Saltses!" Granddad puffed as he coiled the chains into the tractor's tool box. Resting on the rear fender, he took out his flask and winked at me merrily. "Winter chills, boy," he said, taking a drink.

"Do you believe all those ghost stories about Mr. Salts's place, Granddad?" I asked. "He seems real weird sometimes!"

"Mind your manners, boy!" Granddad scolded. "Mr. Salts is a good friend of mine. And, yes, I do believe he experiences presences on his farm."

I rolled my eyes, pretending that I was checking the position of the storm clouds, but I wasn't fooling Granddad. He knew I didn't put much stock in the Donnelly hauntings.

"Never mind about that stuff now!" he growled as he took another swig of medicine. "Let's get back home!"

Soon the whole family was gathered in my grandparents' kitchen. The old wood stove blasted its warmth around us. Granddad dropped more logs into the wood box and slid into his favourite rocker, while Grandma bustled around the kitchen as she prepared cups of English tea and hot chocolate.

"You're the best," Jennifer said as she scooped fluffy marshmallows from the top of her frothing chocolate. "And oatmeal raisin cookies, too. You rock, Grandma!"

Grandma blushed. "Thank you, dear!"

She passed other refreshments to Dad, Mom, and Granddad. "More of your medicine again, dear?"

"Medicine? What medicine?" Granddad grumbled as he stirred an extra teaspoon of sugar into his tea.

He looked at me with annoyance, but I shrugged helplessly. We both smiled. After finishing my hot chocolate, I moved to the opposite side of the kitchen and sat at the long harvest table. The local Lucan paper lay scattered across its polished surface. Idly, I scanned the front page, then stopped at a headline near the bottom of the page.

OLD SCHOOLHOUSE RANSACKED!

Late last night Constable Howard from the Lucan detachment of the Ontario Provincial Police received an anonymous call regarding a possible break-in at the old Biddulph SS

74 School on the Roman Line. The caller, not wishing to be identified, claimed he saw flashlights around the outside of the building. The source then saw shadows enter the darkened schoolhouse.

Creeping closer, the witness saw a small burning firepit in the middle of the dirt floor and heard angry voices rising steadily in serious quarrelling. During a mild scuffle, one of the intruders kicked a burning log into a pile of oily rags. When a larger fire erupted, the informant fled the scene and called the police.

Upon his investigation, Constable Howard did find evidence of an attempted break-in and remnants of a small fire inside the building. After its closure, the school became a private storage shed. According to the owner, none of his property was missing.

Constable Howard attributed the break-in to young midnight frolickers investigating the local myths of midnight ghostly sightings along the Roman Line. Promising regular surveillance, Constable Howard considered the case closed.

"Hey, Granddad!" I called out. "Did you read about this break-in at the schoolhouse?" I leaned back from the table as Jennifer bent over my shoulder to read the article herself.

"Wonder who called it in," Jennifer said. "Says here they didn't find anyone. Any clues, Granddad?"

"Some local punks!" Granddad muttered. "Andrew Smith and his gang of bullies, no doubt."

I glanced at Jennifer. Then we both stared at Granddad as he hunched into his rocking chair and scowled at his steaming cup of tea. We both knew Granddad could be cranky, but we'd never heard him speak so harshly of young people before.

"Now, George," Grandma cautioned, "you can't be sure those boys were there. After all, Andrew's grandparents are quite respected in Lucan, and I'm sure they wouldn't tolerate that kind of behaviour from their grandson."

"Him and his gang of White Boys!" Granddad snorted. "Punks, all of them! Strutting around town with white floppy laces in their black boots!"

"George!" Grandma scolded.

"White Boys?" I said questioningly, but Granddad didn't bother to elaborate.

Grandma sighed. "You've started, George, so you might as well finish."

"Well?" Jennifer prodded. She, too, wanted to know more and waited for Granddad to speak.

"The White Boys," Granddad began, "was the name of a Catholic secret society that had its origins in Ireland a few centuries ago. The members strongly supported the teachings of the priests and the doctrines of the church. Anyone not fully following the dictates of the pope and the Catholic Church was excluded. Those people became known as Blackfeet and often suffered persecution from the White Boys."

"Blackfeet?" I mused.

"That's how you get the name Black Donnellys, Black O'Reillys, or Black O'Tooles," Granddad said. "Any family not fully supporting the Catholic Church or who fraternized with the Protestants had the name Black attached to them."

"So the Donnellys weren't evil?" I asked.

"No," Granddad said, "I wouldn't say that. When it came to drinking and fighting, they could beat the best of them. But I also think they weren't popular because they had friends and did business with everyone in the community, particularly the Protestant Irish."

Grandma coughed. We knew she wanted Granddad to stop, otherwise he'd go on for hours.

Taking the hint, Granddad said no more, and Jennifer and I let the subject drop. After tea Dad made a cell phone call to the movers in their truck. Poor winter visibility and icy road conditions had forced them to pull into St. Marys and stay the night. They promised to arrive early the next morning. We decided to stay the night with Granddad and Grandma. I hoped Jennifer and I would find out more about Andrew Smith. Maybe Lucan would turn out to be more exciting than I'd thought.

The storm tapered off as the night progressed. Granddad snored peacefully in his reclining chair, while Mom and Grandma chatted quietly as they shared their knitting before the living-room fire. Dad invited me to watch the NHL hockey game — Detroit versus Toronto — but I declined, which seemed to disappoint him.

Jennifer nudged me. "If you won't watch hockey, come and play cribbage with me."

I frowned. My earlier good mood had been replaced with the crushing awareness that I was stuck in Lucan whether I liked it or not. However, Jennifer ignored my brooding silence and set up the cribbage board on the kitchen table, loudly banging and shuffling the cards.

"Give it a rest," she said.

"What are you talking about, Stilts?"

She blushed as she carelessly tossed cards to me. "Give Dad a break. He's only trying to do his best for us. I didn't want to come here, either, you know."

I hadn't realized that Jennifer hated this move, too. Quietly, I organized my cards. Jennifer sorted her hand and threw in her two cribbage cards. The first hand played out quickly, and Jennifer pegged sixteen points to my eight. She tossed the deck to me, and it scattered across the table in my direction. I shuffled and dealt the next hand.

"I miss Sam," I whispered. "Dad had no right to bust up our friendship."

"It isn't busted up, Jason. He's my friend and I miss him, too. We just have to work harder at staying close friends, that's all."

"Yeah, right."

I waited with a sneering comeback for her next crack about making new friends in Lucan, but Jennifer kept her focus on her cribbage hand. In short order she beat me again.

"Best three out of five," I said.

Losing to Jennifer did nothing to improve my foul mood. I won the next hand but lost the series by two points in the fourth game. "Enough! I give up!" Without another word I stomped off to the bathroom.

Chapter 4

By the next morning, the storm had stopped. The public works department had worked throughout the night to clear the local roads, and our family easily followed the movers down the Roman Line and into Lucan.

Our new house stood one block off the main street. It was a tall three-storey red brick house that dated back a hundred years or so. Dad had agreed to rent at first, just in case things didn't work out for us in Lucan. Even this small gesture of compromise did nothing to pacify me. The owner had generously ploughed the driveway leading to the stone-blocked garage, and he had shovelled the walk up to the wooden steps of the front porch. Dad drove the car into the narrow lane.

"Here it is!" he said, waiting for our reaction.

Jennifer and I stared through the frosted windows of the car and had to blink away the sunlight that glared in our eyes.

"What did I tell you, Jason?" Dad said. "Every cloud has its silver lining."

I knew he was trying to make us feel better about our new home, but I rebuffed him with a rude huff, got out of the car, slipped, and fell headfirst into a snowdrift. Wiping the melting snow from my neck and coughing on a mouthful of flakes that caught in the back of my throat, I shivered and muttered under my breath.

Jennifer giggled as she pushed past me. "Serves you right!"

I scrambled after her, not wanting to let her have the last word. "If I hear him say that again —"

"Jason, look at this place!" Jennifer said suddenly.

I slammed into her back and nearly landed in the drift a second time. Catching my balance, I gazed straight up at the towering facade of the old house. The second and third storeys seemed to stretch forever to the tall pointed gable that framed the single semicircle window on the attic floor. The wide windows, with their tall white shutters on either side, added to the hugeness of the place. Even the white wooden pillars at the entrance of the front porch appeared overpowering to anyone daring to approach.

"Well, what do you think?" Dad asked.

We hadn't heard him approach, and we both jumped at his sudden appearance. Neither Jennifer nor I answered him.

"Hey!" another voice called out.

All three of us turned toward the shouted greeting from the street. At the end of the walk stood a heavy-set teenager. His hands were shoved into the deep pockets of a short leather jacket, and his collar was pushed up to keep the wind from his neck. He had no winter boots, only high-top black leather boots with the white laces undone and the tongues hanging out. The newcomer wore torn blue jeans that sported unrecognizable pen doodles over the front thighs. He bobbed and stamped to ward off the cold. His gelled hair was spiked in frozen tangles, and a mist enveloped his head — part breath but mostly smoke that drifted from a smouldering cigarette dangling from his bottom lip.

"My name's Smith. Andrew Smith. I live at the end of the street in the yellow brick house."

None of us replied. I stared at the teen's white laces. Was this the same Andrew Smith Granddad had mentioned?

Dad spoke first. "Nice to meet you, Andrew Smith."

He coughed. "Yeah, well, gotta go. This cold's a bummer."

Jennifer giggled as Smith scuttled up the street. He skidded on an icy patch of snow and scrambled frantically to regain his balance. When he flipped away his half-finished cigarette, he looked back at us one more time and I glimpsed the slight scowl he flared at Jennifer. I stepped closer to her side, and Smith continued his hasty retreat from the winter chill.

"Nice guy," Jennifer said. "Come on, Jason! Let's race to see who gets the best bedroom."

"Here, Jen, catch!" Dad tossed the keys to Jennifer as she impatiently rattled the front doorknob. I leaped to intercept the pass and tripped over the drooping buckles of my boots. Jennifer squealed with delight as she caught the keys, opened the door, and rushed inside.

"Geez!" I said as I came into the front hall behind Jennifer and gaped at the high-domed ceiling.

"Oh, Tom!" Mom sighed when she joined us. "It's beautiful! How did you find it?"

"I didn't, Ellen. My dad saw the ad in the paper and set everything up. You really like it?"

I followed Jennifer into the living room. Tucked into the curved corner of one wall, I spied a fireplace. Jennifer's eyes danced at the thought of our first family fire. Large sliding double doors separated the living room from a wide dining room that basked in the sunlight streaming through tall triple windows.

"Come on, Jason!" Jennifer urged.

I sped after her. She laughed as I tried to bull ahead in

the race for the polished wood spiral staircase. Stumbling on the first step, I let Jennifer pass me on the dash for the top of the stairs.

"This room's mine!" she hollered.

I tripped again on the last stair and plunged into the bedroom at the head of the stairs. "No way!" I protested. "This has got to be the largest room in the house. It's got two sets of corner windows and a large walk-in closet."

"It's not the biggest. Mom and Dad's bedroom next door is larger. The bathroom's down the hall. It's completely renovated with a Jacuzzi no less! And there's another sitting room next to that."

I peered into that room. It was about half the size of the other two — long and narrow. There wasn't enough space in it for my double bed, but it was just right for the old couch, two chairs, and our smaller colour TV. "Where's my room?" I asked, my voice almost whiny.

"Over there," Jennifer said.

Her mocking laugh angered me as I stormed down the hall to the half-opened door at the other end. I pushed it open and looked in. "This is just a square box! Who could live in here?"

It really was a tiny square box with only one window looking out on the street and a miniature closet in one corner. The closet door blocked the light from the window when it was opened.

"It's the only room left," Jennifer insisted.

"That's not fair!" I objected, pushing past my sister. Pausing in the hallway, I searched for a place to be alone and away from the people who were slowly ruining my life. I grabbed the last door handle and slammed the door against the top banister post.

"Everything all right up there?"

"It's okay, Mom!" Jennifer said.

"No, Jennifer!" I snapped. "It's not!" I clomped up the darkening stairway to the attic and found myself calming down as the cold pierced my light sweatshirt. Carefully, I felt my way up the steps and finally shuffled my foot over a large, flat surface. Thinking I must have reached the top, I crept forward. When I halted, I grabbed at a thin strand of something that hit me in the face. A light snapped on, and I blinked, then noticed I was holding a string attached to a bare light bulb. "This must be the attic," I whispered to myself.

My breath misted in the damp cold as I surveyed the room's heavy arched beams towering over my head and noted the giant cobwebs dangling from the corners and the thick layers of dust coating the old wooden floor. "What was that?" I croaked.

Fleeting shadows danced everywhere. I spied another door on the far side of the attic and rushed through it. Slamming it shut, I struggled to control my heavy breathing. The sun cast dim light through the quarter-pie window. I fumbled along the wall on both sides of the door and found a light switch. Turning it on, I discovered I was in a smaller bedroom.

It was warmer here than out in the main part of the attic. Apart from the single light and the small window, there was a tiny closet along the far wall. The room was stale and musty and had obviously been closed down for a long time. Still, it was larger than the square box downstairs. I studied the gaudy floral wallpaper. Its faded yellow, pink, and blue did nothing for me. But then again the room was private … and away from parents and Jennifer.

"This will be my room!" I declared.

I moved over to the window and scratched at the layers of dirt and frost. I had a clear view of the street. Under the lamppost on the far corner outside stood a lone person. I watched as he slowly turned and flipped the collar of his leather jacket around his neck. Casually, he flicked away a cigarette butt and pulled a long comb through gelled hair.

"Andrew Smith!" I dropped away from the window as he glanced up at me. *I bet that guy gets to do a lot of things on his own,* I thought. *He's certainly someone I should get to know better.*

"Jason!" a voice called out from the main part of the attic.

I snapped out of my daydream at the sound of Jennifer's voice. Not wanting to surrender my privacy too quickly, I didn't reply.

"Stop fooling around, Jason," she pleaded. "It's dark out here. Where are you?"

"Right here!" I said, moaning throatily as I leaned against the door jamb of my new bedroom and made the kinds of noises I imagined ghosts uttered.

Jennifer shrieked, and I chuckled.

Chapter 5

During the weekend, we unpacked our belongings and set up our new house. Jennifer rarely spoke to me after the fright I'd given her in the attic. I sulked on my own and spoke only when I needed something. Mom and Dad argued against my move to the attic.

"It's winter," Mom protested. "You'll freeze up there, Jason."

"I will not!" I growled. "There's the electric base heater and the steam radiators. Besides, the room's insulated. You said so yourself, Dad."

I knew I had won when Dad shrugged and blushed at Mom's scowl. She shuffled off while Dad and I spent the rest of the morning connecting the electrical wiring for the baseboard heaters in the house.

Monday arrived soon enough, and it was time to go back to school. I stumbled down from my attic perch and slumped into a chair at the breakfast table. "Milk! Where's the milk?" I growled.

Jennifer grinned. "And good morning to you, too, Mr. Personality."

"Don't start with me, *Stilts*."

Mom banged the milk pitcher on the table, settling our tiff. Then she gave us one of her patented warning stares. She didn't get upset with us often, but both Jennifer and I knew when to quit squabbling.

"How did you sleep?" Mom asked us as calm returned to the table.

"Great, Mom!" Jennifer said. "How about you, Jason? Are you warm enough in your cubbyhole?" She peered over the rim of her juice glass.

I didn't dignify her teasing with an answer, but merely grinned through a milky moustache and drooling mouthful of Cheerios.

Actually, I hadn't slept well at all. There had been a constant pinging through the old steam pipes that heated the radiators, and I'd tossed anxiously at every creak of the floorboards, not to mention the hollow footsteps I'd heard outside my bedroom door. I remembered slamming the door hard when I'd thought I'd seen a faint shadow step into the dim moonlight shining through the attic window. And I'd felt a damp chill — even colder than the drafts that whistled constantly about the attic.

"Where's Dad?" I asked quickly, wanting to change the subject.

"He left early this morning," Mom said. "He had an appointment with Bob Jones, his editor."

"Bob Jones?" Jennifer murmured. "That's the guy who wrote the story about the break-in at the schoolhouse, isn't it?"

"That's right," Mom said. "But you two will be late for your first day at your new school if you don't hurry. Your dad left half an hour ago, and I have to drive to London to meet my new nursing supervisor at the University Hospital."

After clearing away and washing the breakfast dishes, Jennifer and I left for school. "Hurry up, Jason! We'll be late!" she told me.

"Big deal! So what, Stilts?" I deliberately slowed my pace and smirked at Jennifer's scowl. Secretly, I hated myself for my on-again, off-again fighting with Jennifer, but I really hoped she'd hurry on her own and leave me to get to school in my own time. But no such luck. She walked silently with me for the next two blocks.

At the dead-end corner of our street, she tugged at my coat sleeve. "Isn't that Andrew Smith taking the shortcut through the park?"

I looked up. "Hey, Andrew!"

As he turned, Andrew stumbled in the shin-deep snow layering the park. The ever-present cigarette dangled from his lower lip, and smoke clouded his vision.

"It's me! Jason Stevens. Remember?"

"Jason!" Jennifer said as she continued to tug on my coat sleeve. "Let's go!"

"Lay off, Stilts!" I yanked my arm away and headed toward the park after Andrew. Just as I was about to cross the street, a shiny grey stretch Cadillac limousine inched its way around the corner. It stopped momentarily to let me cross. I teetered on the side of a snowbank to let the Caddie purr past me. Then it stopped, and the rear passenger window inched down, revealing a pair of mirrored sunglasses.

The owner of the glasses appeared to be in his late twenties or early thirties. His jet-black hair was slicked back close to his head. A large cigar protruded from a heavily moustached mouth, and the hand that reached up to flick ash out the window sported a flashy gold wrist bracelet set with diamonds. Slowly, the window rolled back up. The driver then honked the horn — one short, loud blast.

Andrew quickly turned toward the signal. A tall, lanky figure exited from the far side of the car. He, too, wore mirrored shades, but not the wide plastic-rimmed type. The wire frames of his glasses balanced neatly on the end of his nose. His hair was blond — long and stringy and past his shoulders. The red bandana he wore did nothing to keep the hair off his face as the wind whipped down the street. The blond guy wore a diamond nose stud and two matching gold earrings in each ear. His face was unshaven, and the stubble on his chin made his face look even more menacing. The blond guy waved to Andrew, who ran clumsily through the deep snow. When he reached the car, he ducked into the open door along with the blond fellow. Before the door even closed, the flashy limousine sped away.

"Cool! Did you see that car Andrew has?"

"That's not his car, Jason!" Jennifer's firm reply only encouraged me to press her further.

"And did you see that bracelet the dude in back was wearing? It must have cost a small fortune."

"Be careful, Jason. I have a feeling those aren't nice people, and I'm willing to bet Andrew Smith is in way over his head."

"Nag, nag, nag!" I taunted. "Stilts, that's all you and the folks do is nag. I just want to meet some new friends." I brushed by her and almost knocked her into the snow.

"Jason!" she called out after me.

I could almost see the tears welling in her eyes, but I didn't care. I just kept walking. The school bell rang as we passed through the wrought-iron gates at the entrance to the circular drive. Jennifer raced to the front of the building, flung the heavy brass-panelled door open, and yanked it closed in my face.

"Nice move, Stilts!" I cried through the thick-wired glass, rubbing my shoulder where the door had banged me and growing even angrier with Jennifer when she didn't even turn to answer. Instead she marched toward the school office, her long auburn hair swaying wildly from shoulder to shoulder. Jennifer walked like that only when she was really ticked off with me; but again I didn't care. When I joined her in the school office, I made a point of sitting three seats away from her.

The head secretary of the school greeted us enthusiastically. A slender, elegant lady with neatly coiffured grey hair, she asked several questions about our home address, previous school, and official transcripts. Jennifer replied in a cheerful, polite manner, but I merely nodded or snorted when asked for confirmation of anything.

Next we met the principal of the school. Mr. Simpson was his name. He wore a well-tailored blue suit. As he approached, his broad shoulders filled the waiting room. He extended a large hand and gripped mine in a firm grasp.

"The Stevenses!" he boomed. "We've been expecting you. A little late, I see. No matter. I'm sure you'll adjust to our ways quickly."

Jennifer blushed and apologized, but I said nothing. Gathering up her backpack and her new class timetable, she followed Miss Lumston out the door. I started after her.

"Stevens!"

I halted. Mr. Simpson was waving me back.

"A brief word if I may."

I followed his nod toward his office. Upon entering, I slouched in one of the leather-bound chairs in front of his desk.

"Sit up, please!" he ordered.

I placed my elbows on the armrests and slowly levered my body into an upright position, then I stared at the brown carpet covering the floor. When Mr. Simpson lowered himself into a swivel chair, I still kept my eyes on the carpet.

"I've read your records and know about your community service and probation," he said.

I shrugged nonchalantly, all the while hoping he hadn't noticed the sweat beading on my brow and the clenching of my fists. I was really scared, but I didn't want him to know that. He waited for some sort of reply from me, but when nothing was forthcoming, he continued.

"We have high expectations at this school, Jason, and punctuality is one of them. But I'm also willing to help where I can. Your records are private. Even Miss Lumston is unaware of your probation. You're welcome at this school, but you must also be prepared to participate in a constructive manner." He waited patiently, and again I said nothing. "Right then! It seems everything to be said has been said. I see Miss Lumston is ready to take you to class. You may go."

I flung my pack over my shoulder and shuffled out of the office. *Nice try, jerk!* I thought to myself. *Nice try!*

Jennifer and I didn't have the same classes. We passed each other in the halls, but I refused to speak to or even acknowledge her. I saw her anger slowly turn to disappointment and then to hurt by the end of the first day of school. When the last bell rang, I jammed my homework into my backpack, slammed my locker door, and started for the back door of the school.

"Jason!"

I recognized Jennifer's voice.

"Going home?"

"Nah, not now, Stilts. See you!"

I left the locker bay, but not before I saw the sudden glistening in Jennifer's eyes. I knew I'd hurt her again and had been doing so repeatedly. We used to be so close, but so much had happened — it was too late to turn back now. Besides, I was still really mad at Mom and Dad. Worse, the teachers at this school were total idiots, and apart from Andrew Smith, the kids here were real nerds. Deep down, though, I knew I was only fooling myself — even Mr. Simpson was only trying to be fair.

Stepping out into the back parking lot, I felt envy overwhelm me when I saw all the students lucky enough to have their own cars. The loud groan of the starting engines in the frosty air thundered across the lot, and the cars' exhausts mixed with the fumes of the lingering buses to blanket the ground with a fine mist. The sharp bite of the polluted air scratched at the back of my throat as I moved away from the line of waiting vehicles and wandered toward the back gate.

Through the scattered fog I saw Andrew hanging out with a small group just outside the rear gate. All of them had the same greased spiked hairstyle as Andrew, not to mention tattered jeans with doodled graffiti, short black leather jackets, and white-laced black boots. They huddled closely in a tight circle. I walked toward them, not knowing what to expect. All backs were turned to me or facing into the circle. No one noticed me.

"Hey, Andrew!" I called out.

Several hard stares greeted me at once as hands fumbled into pockets. A red bill drifted slowly to the ground — it was a fifty! Its owner swooped it up and jammed the money into his jacket pocket. Unnoticed at first, I also spied a small plastic-wrapped package on the ground in the centre of the group. It contained greenish-brown flakes. Andrew saw my startled gaze and hurriedly snatched up the fallen packet.

"Dumb idiots!" he growled, jabbing one of his buddies in the ribs. "What do you want, kid?"

"Yeah, dork!" one of the others snarled. "Get lost!"

Everyone in the group split up and wandered off, singly or in pairs. Andrew stayed behind. "Don't ever sneak up on us like that again!" Then he, too, shambled off.

I stood in shock. What had I done? Why were those guys so nervous? They were all dimwits — even Andrew and his pals. Angrily, I kicked a dirty lump of snow that had dropped from a car fender and stomped toward home. My sullen mood didn't improve when I nearly slipped on the icy stairs and then found the front door locked. I rattled the doorknob and banged on the windowpane.

"Hey, Stilts! Open up!" I yelled, watching as Jennifer came out of the living room and wandered down the hall to the kitchen. "Hey, Jennifer!" I pounded on the door again, fuming as she walked back to the front door slowly.

"Come on!" I shouted. "Let me in!"

She fiddled with the lock, then started to open the door. Before she could get the door fully open, I heaved it aside and pushed her behind it.

"Hey!" Jennifer gasped. "Watch it!"

She closed the door and slapped the sleeve of my bulky coat, then raced to the top of the stairs and slammed her bedroom door. I kicked off my boots in the middle of the hall and threw my coat over the knob at the end of the banister. Then I flopped into the overstuffed armchair in the living room and propped my feet on the coffee table. Fidgeting with the television remote, I wondered what to do next, then idly picked up a copy of the local newspaper. Displayed in the bottom right corner in bright pink was a headline: LCBO LOOTED AGAIN!

I skimmed the short article. Thieves had robbed the local liquor store early on Sunday morning. A small amount of alcohol — no money — was missing. This theft was one of several that had occurred recently in the Lucan area. OPP Constable Doug Howard suspected the thefts involved local youths wanting to raise money from a small bootlegging operation to fund their drug buys. The article also stated that an increase in drug sales had occurred in the area.

I stared at the article for several seconds, then smiled. Local youths robbing liquor stores? Selling stolen liquor? Increased drug sales? This was Lucan? Dad sure knew how to pick them. Then I wondered if Andrew Smith had anything to do with all of this.

Chapter 6

Later that night Mom and Dad arrived home at the same time. I waved a lazy hello from the living room and then they disappeared into the kitchen. Overhearing snatches of their conversation, I learned that Mom's day at University Hospital had gone well. She enjoyed her new staff and related well with her immediate supervisor. Then, as Dad began to discuss his day, the hum of chatter became softer, so I got up and leaned around the large open entranceway to the kitchen so I could hear better. Dad was talking about the liquor store robbery, which he had been assigned to cover. He spoke about the grey Cadillac limo that roamed Lucan's streets, and its two strange occupants, who loitered at the entrance of the high school and on the village's main drag.

"That must be the same car we saw today!" Jennifer said behind me suddenly.

I jumped, then turned around. "Are you spying on me?"

"You're one to talk. What are you doing? Spying on Mom and Dad?"

She had a point.

"Where?" another voice demanded.

We looked toward the kitchen whose doorway was now filled by our father. "Where … what?" I sputtered.

"Where did you see that grey Cadillac limo?"

"Like you said, Dad," Jennifer replied, "we saw it near the entrance of the high school. But take it easy. Jason and I only *saw* the car. Nothing else."

"Sorry, Jen." Dad said, his voice a little less on edge. "What happened exactly?"

"Nothing much really," Jennifer said.

I seethed quietly. "Keep quiet, Jen!"

But she didn't. "It passed us on the way to school, and a strange guy with long blond hair called Andrew Smith over to the car. He got in and they drove away."

"Is Andrew the scruffy boy we met outside the house when we moved in?" Mom asked.

"I was afraid of that," Dad said. "His name came up when I talked to Doug Howard this afternoon."

Mom laughed. "I've heard that name a lot lately. You don't mean little Dougie, the one who went to high school with us?"

"The same," Dad said, chuckling. "He joined the OPP about fifteen years ago, right after high school. He's been working in the Lucan area for the past five years."

"I'd like to see him again," Mom said. "It's been a long time."

"Well, you won't have to wait long," Dad said. "He's coming over right after supper this evening. Partly about Jason's probation, I'm afraid."

With that the conversation ended abruptly. The rattle of pans echoed from the kitchen as Mom and Dad scurried to prepare our supper, while Jennifer and I headed back to the living room.

"Way to go, Stilts," I hissed. "You just had to tell them, didn't you?"

"Jason, I …"

Jennifer blushed, then raced up the stairs and banged the door to her room closed. I thumped up to my attic bedroom and blasted my stereo until supper.

A little later supper passed in unusual silence with only mumbled requests to pass bread or butter. I cleared the dishes from the table, hoping to avoid the visit from the OPP officer. Then, to my dismay, the doorbell clanked hollowly and the windowpane rattled under a gentle tap.

"That must be Doug," Mom said, bustling behind me with an armful of dishes. I had no chance for escape up the back stairs. "Get the door please, Jason. I'll put on tea and serve dessert."

I shuffled to the door and yanked it open. A man wearing the OPP's regulation uniform — grey Stetson, dark blue coat, and dark blue pants with a lighter blue stripe — stood before me. He was of medium height, yet stocky and thick-chested. When he removed his wide-brimmed hat, his light brown hair stuck to his head in a perfect ring. His broad smile showed a set of even white teeth, while his extended hand revealed a thick, powerful wrist and forearm. The man's handshake was firm, but not tight or gripping. "Doug Howard," he said. "And you must be Jason."

I left him standing there for a moment. Then Dad appeared. "Invite him in, Jason. He's an old friend."

I stepped aside to allow Constable Howard to enter.

"Jennifer! Ellen!" Dad called. "Can you come here for a moment, please?"

I moved closer to the banister to let Mom through to greet our guest.

"Dougie Howard!" Mom said cheerily. "How nice to see you again." She gave him a friendly hug and smiled a cheery welcome. "You've already met Jason, and this is my daughter, Jennifer."

"They both look just like you, Ellen. Certainly not the

ugly gorilla you married."

They all laughed. Slowly, I turned and started up the staircase.

"Not so fast, young man!" Dad said. "Come join us in the living room."

For the next half-hour I listened to memories of old high school football games won or lost by Doug and Dad. Mom had attended many of the games they'd played and had even had a crush on Constable Howard early in their high school years, starting with summer beach parties at Grand Bend on Lake Huron.

Eventually, there was a lull in the conversation, and Dad said softly, yet seriously, "Jennifer, your mother and I need to talk to Doug for a moment. I'm afraid it's official business."

Jennifer caught on. "No problem, Dad. I have a ton of homework." She stood and went upstairs to her bedroom.

I grimaced at the thought of studying, but at least that was better than staying. I, too, made a move to go.

"Jason, we need you here," Dad said.

I stopped midway out of my chair, then sank back into it. I said nothing but glowered at Dad.

"It's not your dad's fault," Constable Howard said, noticing the look on my face. "Yes, I came to visit your folks as my old friends, but I'm also on duty this evening and have some official business with you. It's about your community service and probation."

I frowned more heavily.

"You're to start your community service this weekend, am I right?"

I nodded slightly, and allowed Constable Howard to continue.

"Your probation officer is Sandy Jones. She's off on maternity leave for the next six months. There's no replacement for her yet. Social Services is short-staffed, and we don't know when counselling will begin. During her absence, you're to check in with me on a regular basis. How's Thursday afternoons at the police station? Say 4:30 p.m.?"

I blinked rapidly and swallowed to clear the lump in my throat. My punishment had finally come. I knew it had to eventually, but I hadn't expected the emotional reaction I was experiencing.

Mom sighed, crossed the room, and sat on the arm of my chair. She placed a warm hand over mine, but I jerked it away. Then I lowered my head, feeling true shame. Covering my face with both hands, I couldn't stop the sobbing that coursed out of me for the first time since my arrest. I heard, rather than saw, Dad and Constable Howard move across the living room to the hall. Their conversation was a series of muffled whispers. The front door closed, and the constable left. Mom wrapped her arms around my shoulders, and despite the instant stiffening in my muscles, she stubbornly continued to hold me.

"Jason, it'll be all right," she said, trying to console me.

Dad reached out, too, but I knocked his hand away, then wriggled out of Mom's embrace. "No, it won't!" I shouted. "You don't get it, do you?"

I raced for the stairs, taking them two at a time until I reached the attic. Not stopping to turn on the light, I stumbled in the dark, lurched against my bedroom door, and heaved it open with one shoulder. I ignored the splintering of wood and charged into the room, flopping onto the bed and burying my sobs in a pillow.

Just as quickly I stopped and peeked out from under the

pillow. Was that my stereo playing? I hadn't turned it on. I glanced at the volume indicator and saw the pulsating line of red dots moving back and forth across its scale. The music wasn't loud, but I could still feel the heavy bass vibrating through the floor as I swung my feet off the bed.

I walked over to the stereo and turned the volume up louder. A piercing squeal followed and then the music skipped from one song to the other. Trying to plug my ears, I fumbled with the volume switch to stop the screech, then slumped against the stereo case, attempting to steady my heavy breathing and calm my thumping heart. But it didn't work.

In a panic I careened toward the door and tried to open it, but it was jammed. I noticed the splinter that ran along the hinge side and saw that the door had come away from its frame. Grasping the doorknob with two hands, I lifted and pulled, and suddenly the door scraped over the warped floorboards and sprang free. I fell with the door against the far wall. Pushing myself free, I stepped out into the darkened main part of the attic. My misted breath swirled around my head, and a damp film clung to my face. I tried to wipe it away. Then I heard a noise — hollow footsteps clumping up the stairs.

"Who … who's there?" But there was no answer.

The steps thudded more raucously as the sound seemed to turn at the landing and come up the final flight. Then I saw it! A faint glow appeared over the rim of the last stair. I froze, and my ears hummed. The glow grew larger, but softened and faded to reveal a human figure.

It was a man — short and broad-shouldered. A thick, dark moustache curled around the corners of his mouth, and a pillbox-style hat covered his head. He wore a white shirt with a round collar and a string tie. His long overcoat stretched below his knees, and his pants seemed too long and bagged untidily over his shiny boots. All his clothes were black. He moved closer.

"Stop! Please stop!" I pleaded.

He advanced slowly. I put my arms straight in front of me in a desperate attempt to ward him off, then screamed when my hands passed through his chest.

"Jason!"

I blinked at the sudden bright light and crawled away from the blinding naked bulb, raising my arm again to protect my eyes.

"It's Jennifer! What's wrong? What happened?"

"Where is he?"

"Where's who, Jason? You're scaring me!"

"Geez, Jen! Didn't you see him? He came up those stairs in a glowing halo. Short guy, bushy moustache, dressed in black. He walked right though me." I stopped when I saw terror growing in Jennifer's widening eyes.

"Jason, there's no one here."

I turned and saw packing boxes stacked in the corner. Cobwebs dangled from the rafters. The single bulb hung from its long electrical cord. I heard the soft drone of my stereo. "But, Jen, he was here. Honest!"

I grasped Jennifer's hand and led her back to my room. As I leaned unsteadily on her, she eased me onto the bed. Lifting my feet under the puffy duvet, she pulled it up to my neck. I heard the clicks of the volume control on my stereo and the light switch by the door. Then there was total blackness as I let myself drift into deep sleep.

The next morning I climbed down the attic stairs and onto the upper landing. I heard whispers and had only one thought. *Not him again!* Then I recognized Jennifer's voice as it came from the phone stand at the foot of the stairs. Sitting on the top step and out of her view, I listened.

"But, Sam," she said, "you've got to come."

I clenched my teeth through the long pause while Sam replied.

"I know we promised we'd come visit you at March break, but I need you here."

I craned my head around the corner post of the banister, then jerked back as Jennifer turned to look up at the ceiling.

"Please, Sam! He's acting really weird. He says he's seeing ghosts in the attic now. He's met some rough kids at school, and I'm afraid he'll skip his probation. Thanks, Sam. I understand." She laughed, probably at one of Sam's dumb one-liners. "Hope the exam goes well."

I waited through another long pause.

"No, Jason doesn't know I called. And I won't tell him. But I'm also going to call Granddad and let him investigate this ghost thing."

I waited a little longer for Jennifer to hang up, then charged down the stairs. "You just had to do it, eh, Stilts? Leave Sam out of this. It's none of his business. You had no right to call him."

Jennifer launched her own attack. "He's not coming. He's had pneumonia and has to study for a makeup exam during March break." She fled toward the kitchen. I followed her and slumped into a chair, trying to calm myself. When I stared at her, she glared back, then quickly ate her breakfast. There were no sarcastic comments about a good night's sleep or teasing about the black rings under my eyes.

"Jason, you don't look well," Mom said, scurrying over

and placing a hand on my forehead. "No temperature, but your eyes are glassy and you look as white as a ghost."

I flinched. "Nothing's wrong, Mom," I said, trying to sound jaunty, but my voice was flat. "I just didn't sleep well last night."

Mom shook her head. "If you say so …" She finished with the toaster, and when she returned with freshly buttered toast, she made one last try. "Maybe you should stay home. I'm on the afternoon shift at the hospital and can stay here until two o'clock this afternoon."

"No, Mom, I'm fine. Really I am." After last night, I just wanted to get out of the house, even if it meant going to school without my homework being done. My toast tasted like cardboard, so I excused myself and gathered my books for school. I left with a muffled "See you!" and headed out the door and down the street toward school.

I didn't hear the soft drone of the car engine over my squeaking footsteps on the dry, hard snow until the grey Caddie was beside me. It stopped, and the window rolled down slowly. The same pair of mirrored sunglasses stared out at me again. The choking puff from a large cigar sailed toward me as the hand with the diamond-studded gold wrist bracelet flicked ash onto the street. A smirk lurked beneath the heavy moustache. "Get in, kid. We need to talk."

I didn't move. Then the opposite passenger door opened, and the blond guy with the red bandana appeared. He came toward me around the end of the car. I lost him for a moment in the exhaust, then tried to bolt but slipped on an icy patch. He grabbed the hood of my coat and held me up.

"When the Boss says 'Get in!' that's what we do!" He steered me roughly back around the rear bumper of the car.

The man with the cigar chuckled. "Easy, J.T. We want

him in one piece."

I stood helplessly as J.T. fumbled with the door handle. I glanced down the street and spotted Jennifer. She walked with her head down, attempting to rebalance her backpack. As J.T. pushed me into the back seat, Jennifer saw me and stopped short. Her mouth opened to call me, but I shook my head and waved her away harshly. Then I plunged headfirst into the car. I landed on a soft leather seat and felt the warmth radiating off them as I smelled the fragrant scent of air freshener.

The Boss snuffed his cigar in the ashtray and flipped the air filter switch to clear the lingering smoke. Two sets of bench seats faced each other. J.T. and I sat on one side and the Boss on the opposite. I took in the mahogany panelling lining the bottom portion of the doors and the low table sitting between the two seats. Plush maroon upholstery covered the walls and ceiling. The Boss lifted the mirrored-glass top of the table.

"Drink, Jason?" He laughed. "Of orange juice?"

The table was actually a portable bar containing a variety of juices, soft drinks, and alcohol. I shook my head.

"Relax!" the Boss snickered. "We're driving you to school."

I shifted nearer to the door. "What do you want?"

"Your cooperation, kid," J.T. snarled, leaning toward me.

"What for?" I said, trying to sound tough, but my voice squeaked, and J.T. laughed.

"We need your help protecting our investment with Andrew Smith," J.T. said.

"What's he got to do with me?"

"Nothing yet. We need a place for Andy to do his

business, somewhere away from your old man and that OPP cop, Howard, so they don't start asking too many questions."

"How do I do that?"

"Easy! You work Saturday evenings at the museum cleaning floors, don't you?"

I said nothing, and J.T. didn't stop. "Right around midnight we need you to open the back door to that storeroom. It's small and well hidden from the street. It'll be a great place for Andy to do business with his clients."

"I can't do it," I said. "I won't do it. I'm on probation."

"So I hear." The Boss fixed me with a stare. "Let me put it this way. You cooperate with us and you stay clean. If not, you might find a surprise package in your locker or backpack. Some Colombian smack — not much, mind you, just enough to get the right people excited. Maybe even your sister, Jenny, could have some, too. You'd like that, wouldn't you?" The Boss chortled harshly.

"It's Jennifer!" I shouted. "And you leave her out of this!" I lunged at the Boss, but J.T. shoved me back into the seat.

"Ah!" the Boss said. "There's Andrew now. He's expecting you."

The driver stopped the limousine at the front entrance of the school, and Andrew opened the rear door for me. "Out, kid! Now!" he growled. As soon as I climbed out, he slammed the door.

Before the car drove away, the window rolled down one more time. The Boss squinted, put his mirrored sunglasses back on his face, and smoothed his well-oiled black hair into place. "I take it we have a deal?"

I dipped my head slightly in mute agreement, and the car sped off. When the bell rang, I scampered after Andrew, who had already reached the front door. I saw Jennifer's reflection in the large glass panel. I hesitated, then stepped into the narrowing gap of the closing door. I didn't wait for her.

Chapter 7

For the next three weeks I followed the Boss's instructions. Each Saturday night at midnight, just before my shift ended at the museum, I answered two raps with one short one on the back door. As instructed, I turned all the lights off except the small forty-watt bulb over the exit sign. The light from lampposts lanced through the small flip-up window. On the first night I fumbled with the keys as I unlocked the back door.

"What took you so long?" Andrew growled when I finally got the door open.

J.T. barged past me and scanned the darkened storeroom. "Good job, kid!" I bristled at the false praise. "Perfect place." He returned to the door and waved at the idling Caddie. The Boss stepped out, puffing on a cigar as he strode toward the storeroom. He draped a long black wool overcoat across one shoulder. As he brushed past me, I detected the sweet odour of pot lingering in his coat. He seemed satisfied.

"Where are they then?" he asked Andrew abruptly.

Andrew glanced at his watch anxiously. "Should be here by now. Honest."

For the first time I watched Andrew squirm. I got a kick out of it.

"No sweat, Boss," J.T. chimed. "Everything's under control. Right, Andrew?"

"It's under control, J.T."

"We'd better leave, Boss," J.T warned. "The Caddie stands out too much and someone might see us."

Following J.T. to the door, the Boss stopped beside me and blew a toxic cloud of cigar smoke in my face. "Don't screw up, either of you!" Then he left.

I locked the door, and the two of us waited. I tried talking with Andrew to pass the time. "Where's the stuff?"

Andrew said nothing, but patted the zippered pocket on his leather jacket and puffed nervously on a cigarette. He butted it on the windowsill and burned his thumb when he heard a loud knock on the door. I threw him the keys.

"It's about time!" Andrew said when he opened the door. "Where have you been, Tyler?"

"None of your business! We're here, ain't we?"

Four other shadows shuffled through the door. I recognized them as the same group I'd seen outside the back entrance of the school. I gaped at the large rolls of bills that appeared from pockets. Andrew carefully counted the money from each purchase.

"Don't trust us, eh?" Tyler sneered. He grabbed Andrew by the jacket collar and drew him closer.

Andrew seized the other kid's wrist and sharply twisted out of the grip. "As much as you trust me! Here's your stuff." He threw the cellophane packages at the buyers. Each clawed the air to catch his stash. "You've got it. Now shove off!"

Stuffing their dope into pockets, they stumbled through the door. I watched Andrew as he sorted and recounted the cash. His hands still shook as he flicked his lighter to fire up another cigarette. "See you later," he growled at me, and left.

I locked the door and returned to my last-minute cleanup of the museum. As I swept the front mats, I tried to convince myself that if I didn't deal or buy, then I wasn't breaking any laws. I resisted the mocking sneers of the Boss and J.T. as they, too, tried to hook me into their drug ring. As long as I fended off the police and kept my dad from doing too much snooping, they seemed happy.

I shook out the mats, then put them back. When I stooped to straighten a corner, I felt cool, moist air tickle the back of my neck. The fluorescent lights flickered, and one went out, then back on again. I stiffened when I heard the sound of running footsteps. "Who's there?" I gasped.

There was no answer. Then the back door started to rattle. Cautiously, I moved toward the storeroom again. "Andrew, is that you?"

Again there was no answer. Stopping to wipe my sticky palms on my jeans, I gripped the doorknob and twisted it. At first it stuck, but with another firm twist and a shove, I staggered into the dark storeroom. An even colder breeze swept across my face, and the small light bulb above the exit popped. The outside door itself was open. I walked forward. Again I heard footsteps. This time they crunched in the cold, dry snow. A thin shadow appeared in the moonlit door frame.

"What do you want?" I bellowed, tightening the grip on the broom handle.

Someone chuckled. "Easy, Jason!"

I recognized that chuckle, and soon caught a whiff of stale pipe tobacco. "Granddad!"

I jumped again as he peered around the door jamb. He knocked the dead ashes from his pipe bowl, removed his fur cap with its large earflaps, and swept stringy grey hair off his forehead.

"You scared me."

"I scared you. What do you think you did to me?" He

quickly pulled the flask from the inside of his coat and took a short swig. "Need to calm my nerves, boy."

"Sure, Granddad, sure."

"What are you doing here, anyway? Your shift ended an hour ago."

I coughed, pretending I was clearing my throat while I thought about what to say. "I got backed up when the lights started to flicker. Then those footsteps — that must have been you."

"Probably," Granddad muttered. "And those lights? The ones over the front door?"

I nodded.

"I've been meaning to fix those."

"But what are you doing here, Granddad?"

He shuffled nervously but didn't reply.

"Granddad?"

"Oh, all right!" he fumed. "Did you feel a drop in temperature or a sudden moisture in the air just now?"

"Yes, I did."

"And those footsteps weren't mine. And those lights? I've checked the circuit breakers three times today and they're fine."

"What are you saying, Granddad?"

"It's him, or her! The ghost! Help me with this equipment."

Before I could protest, Granddad disappeared out the door. I heard him rummaging in the back of his old van and gawked when he returned with several steel poles, metal dish scanners, and yards of electrical wire.

"What's all that?" I asked.

"It's my EMF reader and thermal scanner. They measure changes in electromagnetic fields and temperature."

"So what?"

Granddad ignored me as he scuttled to hook up his wires and position the scanning dishes. In a matter of minutes he had a jungle of electrical equipment set up in the back of the museum just outside the storeroom. "Think I'm crazy, eh? Watch this." He flipped two switches and twisted several knobs as I stared at the flickering needles. "See there!" he hooted.

I stretched over his shoulder to get a better look. One of the needles climbed steadily, while the other dropped quickly. I felt a sudden, sharp chill in the air and a return of the sticky moisture around my neck. Then several sparks zipped across the maze of wires. Granddad fell back against me, and we both tumbled to the floor, bringing the steel support poles for the scanners on top of us. All was black for several seconds, then the fluorescent lights flickered back on.

"Did you see that, Jason?"

"What was it?"

"The ghost!" Granddad cackled. "He was here. He likes to play tricks with electricity."

"But, Granddad, how do you know for sure?"

"The dials, boy. The energy level's way up, and didn't you feel the cold? The temperature dropped like a rock. I knew it!"

I said nothing, deciding to let my grandfather have his moment of glory. For the next half-hour I helped him roll up his wires, collapse his scanners, and return everything to the van. He perched on the back of his bumper and again took out the flask. "I'll wait here. Get your coat and lock up. I'm driving you home."

"It's okay, Granddad. Dad's coming to get me."

"Not tonight. He got called out on an assignment. And your mother's working the night shift at the hospital. I told them I'd get you home."

I shrugged. "Sure! Thanks, Granddad."

Darting back through the storeroom and into the museum to the main power box, I flicked the master switch, and the dim emergency lights came on. Not wanting to stay around any longer than I had to, I ran to the back exit of the storeroom. I fumbled with the locks, and after the final click, closed the door and latched it securely. Just as I turned to leave, I halted.

"Granddad!" I cried, pointing shakily at the wall. Just under the exit light we both read the word MURDERED!

Neither of us heard the crunch of car tires on snow, nor did we notice headlights streaking down the outside alley. Then we heard the short shriek of a police siren and covered our eyes against the flashing red and blue lights.

"Evening, Jason. Mr. Stevens. Everything all right?" Constable Howard grinned through his half-open passenger window. "Didn't mean to startle you."

I froze, but Granddad quickly stepped into the conversation. "I think you ought to see this, Doug."

I glanced at Granddad. The last thing I wanted was Constable Howard lurking around the museum's back door late at night.

"What's up, Mr. Stevens?" Constable Howard left his car running in the cold and followed Granddad into the storeroom.

"Coming, Jason?" Granddad asked.

I ran after them and bumped into Constable Howard as he shone his flashlight over the red lettering on the wall.

"Easy, Jason!" the officer said. "You seem real nervous all of a sudden."

I said nothing and let Constable Howard finish his

inspection.

Finally, he flicked off his light. "See anyone hanging around the back alley tonight, Jason?"

I shook my head.

"Me, neither," Granddad said when the constable looked to him.

"Probably pranksters," Constable Howard said. "Over the past two Saturday nights, Jason, I noticed that the outside door was left open. When I turned around at the end of the alley to come back for a second look, though, the door was closed. Think anyone might have sneaked in while you weren't looking?"

Granddad scowled at me when he heard Constable Howard's question. I flushed and said, "I … I sometimes leave the door open for a few minutes while I get the mats from the museum. I shake them out the door here. I don't think anyone could get in during that short time."

The constable turned to Granddad again. "Any other damage? Anything missing, Mr. Stevens?"

"No damage, and all the artifacts seem to be in the museum stands," Granddad said. "I can take a look first thing tomorrow and let you know for sure."

"Good idea," Constable Howard said. "I'll record the incident in my log and wait for your report. I'm going to patrol this alley regularly for the next few weeks, just to be sure. I've seen some of the local boys skulking around lately, and I want to make certain nothing's going on."

My weakened knees nearly buckled, and I felt sweat dripping on my forehead. I said nothing as Constable Howard bid us good night and drove off in his cruiser.

Granddad sighed when the constable was gone. "Thanks for not saying anything about the scanners and the ghosts!

You all right, Jason? You look pale."

I shrugged.

"Let's close up for now and get you home."

The drive in Granddad's old van was cold. The blasting heater couldn't keep up with the freezing drafts that curled through the rusted seams in the floorboards. Granddad swore constantly as he scraped the frost off the inside of the windshield. As soon we pulled into our driveway and stopped, I thanked Granddad, hurried out of the van, and rushed toward the front door of our house. I wanted to get away and be alone.

"Jason!" Granddad called.

I stopped but didn't turn back.

"Keep that back door at the museum closed from now on, will you, son? I don't want any more unwanted guests than we already have."

I waved at him, then hustled up the front steps, wondering if Granddad suspected what was really going on in the museum. Entering the house quietly, I found everything perfectly still. The lights on the upper landing and in the kitchen stayed on for any of us coming home late. I left them on for Mom and Dad and didn't even bother to raid the refrigerator. I was too tired tonight and was suffering from a case of jangled nerves.

On my way up to the attic, I peered through Jennifer's open doorway. She lay on two pillows with a collapsed book in her lap. Her chin rested on her chest as she slept. Pangs of guilt prickled my conscience over my treatment of her, but I convinced myself that I was actually protecting both of us from Andrew's threats.

Not bothering to turn out her light, I sneaked up the attic stairs to my own bedroom and closed the now-repaired door tightly. I'd had enough of ghostly visitors for one night and tumbled into bed gratefully.

Chapter 8

With a jolt, I awoke to muffled voices and banging doors.

"Jason! Jason!" I heard Jennifer call out, panic in her voice. "Come down quick!"

Throwing back the covers and lurching through the darkness of the attic, I plunged through the door at the bottom of the attic stairs. "What now?" I gasped.

"It's Granddad! He's in the hospital. Mom just called. He arrived in emergency about a half-hour ago."

"But … but he just dropped me off not five minutes ago. What could have happened that fast?"

"Not five minutes ago," Jennifer snapped. "Try five hours ago. It's six-thirty in the morning!"

I jiggled my head to shake off the drowsiness. I was usually the one to take charge in a crisis, but this time Jennifer was in control. "Does Dad know?" I asked. "We have to get to the hospital."

"Yes, Dad knows, and no, we're not going to the hospital. Mom said Granddad's still in recovery and won't be ready for visitors until this afternoon at the earliest. We're to stay here and wait."

I plunked down on the bottom stair. Jennifer went to the kitchen, rattled around in the refrigerator, and returned with a glass of orange juice. Not offering me any, she went to the living room and turned on the TV. I heard the annoying opening music of *Canada AM* and cupped my head in my hands to relieve the groggy morning headache, blocking out the blaring television until I heard the beginning of the local news.

"Police and firefighters are still at the scene of a mysterious barn fire on the Roman Line. The property belonged to Mr. Ted Stevens, who was rushed to University Hospital in London with severe smoke inhalation and burns to his hands and arms. He suffered no life-threatening injuries and is expected to recover fully. Mrs. Ellen Stevens said her husband, Tom, Ted's son, left their home to quell a fire that had erupted in the barn. She immediately called 911. Upon their arrival, they rescued Ted Stevens from the burning building. The fire destroyed the barn and most of its equipment, but the firefighters saved the house. Fire Chief Lewis told us that the cause at this time is unknown, but the investigation will continue. This is Simon Case reporting ..."

I leaned against the living-room doorway and jumped at the sound of shattering glass when Jennifer dropped her orange juice on the hardwood floor. Looking across at her huddled form in the overstuffed chair, I saw she had buried her face in her knees and was clutching her arms tightly around her body. Her long auburn hair fell over her heaving shoulders.

Swallowing the lump in my throat, I moved to her side, sat on the arm of the chair, and put an arm around her. She turned her face into my chest and continued to sob. I vaguely heard the doorbell, but only moved when there was a loud rap on the front door. Prying myself away from Jennifer, I went over to the door and pulled it open. "Constable Howard!" I said, surprised. "What are you doing here?"

"Your mom and dad wanted me to drop by to make sure

you kids are all right. I guess you've heard the news?"

"Just now over *Canada AM*." Constable Howard stared over my shoulder, and at the same time I felt Jennifer's head rest against my back.

"Your grandfather's just fine," the constable said. "He's still in shock and is sedated to numb the pain of the burns. You can visit him later this afternoon."

Jennifer sighed. "Do you know what happened?" She was still leaning against my shoulder, but her voice seemed steady and her sobbing had stopped.

"We have no real proof," the constable said reluctantly, "but early signs indicate it may have been arson."

"Arson!" Jennifer and I both gasped. "Who? How do you know that?" we both said at once.

"I shouldn't be telling you any of this," Constable Howard said, "but I found fresh tracks in the snow leading across your grandfather's field. I followed them for about a hundred yards and discovered an old kerosene can and a leather boot. The boot had white laces."

"Andrew Smith," I muttered. "I knew he'd do this."

Jennifer stared at me in shocked silence, and I wished I'd kept my mouth shut.

"Anything you want to tell me?" Constable Howard asked.

"Nothing," I mumbled. "It's just that Andrew Smith and his buddies all wear those boots with white laces."

"I'm aware of that," Constable Howard said. "We also have a fresh footprint in the snow and will see if it matches any of those boys' boots. Meanwhile I'd rather you not mention any of this to your friends." He paused and looked deep into my eyes.

My face flushed. "Yes, sir!"

"Good! I'm off to see if the doctor will give me permission to see your grandfather. Stay home until your parents get back."

He let himself out the front door before Jennifer or I had a chance to say anything else. I headed toward the kitchen.

"Jason!" Jennifer called after me, but I ignored her.

"Did you leave any orange juice, Stilts?" I asked as I searched the shelves in the fridge.

"Jason!"

I had no choice but to pay attention this time as Jennifer grabbed the collar of my shirt and spun me around to face her. My face burned. I said nothing. I just stood there.

"You're not going to tell me, are you? I know something's going on with you and Andrew Smith. Are you into drugs? Did he set the fire at Granddad's farm?"

She shoved the juice container into my chest. I didn't retaliate when the sticky orange juice splashed down the front of my shirt. I wanted to call Jennifer back, but the moment had passed.

We didn't talk to each other for the rest of the morning. Jennifer pretended to do her homework in her room. With the thump of books on the floor and the crash of closet doors, I knew she wasn't doing homework. She was mad — really mad. I decided to stay downstairs and idly flip channels from one sports and entertainment channel to another. I was in the kitchen when I heard the front door open.

"I'm home!" Mom called out.

"Mom? Dad?" I heard Jennifer cry from her room.

I rushed out to greet them. Even talking to Mom and Dad was better than the silent treatment I was getting from my sister. "How's Granddad?" I asked, colliding with Jennifer at the bottom of the stairs. She jabbed me in the ribs and coldly pushed me aside.

"He's resting in recovery still," Mom said.

"When will he come home?" Jennifer asked.

Mom collapsed into an overstuffed chair and stretched her long legs out in front of her.

Jennifer placed a fluffy pillow behind her head and lifted her feet onto a stool. "Sorry, Mom, I know you're tired."

"It's okay, Jen," Mom said. "We're all concerned about your grandfather."

"A cup of tea, Mom?" I asked, trying to be helpful.

"Thanks! That would be nice, dear."

I left for the kitchen and listened as Mom and Jennifer continued talking.

"Your grandfather will be released from the hospital this afternoon. Your dad and Grandma are with him now. Constable Howard is talking to Granddad and then your dad will discharge him. He and Grandma will be coming here for the next few days. She's too exhausted to look after him on her own."

"Constable Howard says the fire might be arson," Jennifer said. "They found footprints in the snow and a boot with white laces. Is it Andrew Smith?"

"No one knows for sure. Until the police make some positive identifications we can't say anything."

My hand shook as I poured the boiling water into the teapot. The cups rattled on the tray as I carried everything into the living room. I felt Jennifer's cold stare before I even walked through the archway.

After having tea, Mom rested for the afternoon in her room. Jennifer and I continued on as before — not talking and staying out of each other's way. Dad didn't come home that night. He stayed at the farm to help Grandma and

Granddad organize their stay with us.

Mom awoke early the next morning. She got the spare room off the upstairs bathroom set up for Grandma. Granddad was to have a special hospital bed that Mom planned to put in the dining room. She had pushed the last dining-room chair out of the way when the doorbell rang.

"Jason! Jennifer!" she called. "Granddad's bed is here. Can you come help?"

Not wanting to say anything really stupid, I stuffed my mouth full of milk and cereal. It didn't even bother me that half of my breakfast was drooling down my chin. Jennifer looked at me in disgust, and I quickly wiped my face.

Jennifer held the door for the delivery men, and Mom led them into the dining room. They set up the bed and mattress in minutes. Mom paid them, and they left before I finished my cereal.

"Great help, Jason!" Jennifer said as she bounded up the stairs to her room.

Again I said nothing. I knew the more I talked, the more Jennifer would try to weasel answers out of me. Eventually, I'd have to tell her, but not now. I needed to find out more about what Andrew Smith was up to.

Our walk to school was the same as every other day. Jennifer stayed a few steps behind me, and we didn't speak to each other. I kept glancing over my shoulder to see if the Caddie would mysteriously appear around a corner, but it didn't. Jennifer and I silently parted company at the front entrance of the school. The rest of the day passed without incident. I saw Andrew several times in the hallways, but passed him with no comment.

That changed, though, during lunch break. I joined the cafeteria line three people behind Andrew and watched as he set his tray down on a window table away from the crowd. After paying for my lunch, I strolled over to his table and took a seat. He seemed startled at first, then sneered.

"What do you want? Can't you see I'm eating lunch?"

I ignored his tough-guy act and blurted, "You burnt my grandfather's barn. We agreed no rough stuff if I did what the Boss asked."

I lunged for Andrew's neck, and both of our lunch trays skidded across the table, crashing in a runny mess on the floor. Andrew's chair tipped over, dragging me with him. I landed on top of him, but he easily flipped me over. He was stronger than I'd thought, and I realized I was outmatched.

"Stop!" Mr. Simpson bellowed, his voice echoing throughout the cafeteria. He easily pushed Andrew aside and plucked me from the floor. "Office now!"

I straightened my crumpled shirt and brushed my pants clean. Andrew left for the office. Just as I was about to follow, Jennifer pulled my arm.

"Jason!" she hissed. "What was that all about?"

At first I wanted to give a smart-aleck reply, then I saw the stark fear in Jennifer's eyes. "I'll explain later, Jen. Go back to class. I'll see you after school."

"Promise?"

"Yeah, I promise."

I really meant it. The time had come to tell someone, and the only person I could trust at the moment was Jennifer.

Andrew and I sat in Mr. Simpson's outer office for over an hour. We could see him through the partly open doorway. He removed his suit coat and rolled up the sleeves of his pinstriped dress shirt, revealing muscular forearms. He was an intimidating man. Several phone calls later he beckoned us into his office.

"Explain!" he ordered before Andrew or I had a chance to completely sit in our chairs.

I gulped. "It's my fault entirely, Mr. Simpson. I accused Andrew of a personal insult and lost my temper. He had nothing to do with it."

"Is that true, Smith?" Mr. Simpson asked.

Andrew didn't look at me. "Just a misunderstanding, that's all, sir. It won't happen again."

"It's over," I agreed.

Mr. Simpson rocked in his spring-loaded chair and pressed his two forefingers against his lips. I was afraid he wasn't going to believe us and would demand more information, but instead he sighed deeply. "Stevens, I know your family's having a tough time right now with the fire and your grandfather's injuries. Your parents don't need a phone call about your fighting in school. So far you've done as I've asked and kept your attendance and grades up at school. I gave Constable Howard a very positive report on your progress. Smith seems to be the victim here, and he's willing to let the matter drop. No damage was done in the cafeteria, and no one was hurt. Stevens, I'm going to let you off with just a warning this time. But both of you consider yourselves on probation. Any more such altercations and there will be serious repercussion. Understand me?"

We both nodded.

"Any questions?"

Andrew and I mumbled, "No, sir."

"All right, off to class now."

We both rose at the same time, but I stepped aside to let Andrew go around my chair and out the door first. In the hall I confronted him again. "If I find out that you set that fire on my grandfather's farm —"

"I had nothing to do with it," he said, leering at me. Then he sauntered down the hallway as if he owned the school.

The rest of the day passed normally. I didn't see Andrew again or speak to Jennifer. At the final bell I jammed my biology text and notes into my backpack and darted from the room even before the teacher finished outlining our homework. I think he may have tried to call me back, but I simply kept walking.

Coming down the hall, I spotted Jennifer at her locker. She turned her back to me as I walked the extra three lockers to my own. I peered at her out of the corner of my eye. Jennifer seemed frozen. She stared at her books. I dropped mine and moved swiftly toward her.

"Jennifer, what's wrong?" No reply. "Are you all right?" I gently turned her toward me, then gasped at the blank expression on her face. She remained mute but shakily handed me a small plastic pouch with brown leaves in it. "Where did you get that?" I whispered, taking the package from her hand and hugging her.

"I don't know where it came from, Jason!" she sobbed. "It was taped to the inside of one of the textbooks I needed for homework."

"Well, well, what do we have here?" It was Andrew. "A tender brother-and-sister moment? How nice!"

I whirled on him. "What is this, Smith? My grandfather's barn and now Jennifer?"

"I don't know what you're talking about, kiddo," Andrew said.

"This, buddy boy!" I snapped, opening my sweaty palm to show him the package.

Andrew grinned and took the bag. He tore open the taped flap, then sniffed the aroma of the leaves. He pinched some of the flakes and dribbled the crumbs back into the bag. "Tobacco! It's just tobacco. Old Dutch, I think."

I tightened my muscles to control my rising temper. "You did this!"

Andrew smirked. "Just a gentle reminder, kiddo. Be careful who you talk to and are seen with. The Boss knows everything."

I watched him swagger away. Speechless, I threw the package in a garbage can.

"What did he mean, Jason?" Jennifer asked.

Her look wasn't angry or threatening, just scared. I knew the time had come. Enough of the guilt-trip routine and tough-boy act. I had to come clean.

Chapter 9

At first we walked home in silence. Neither of us wanted to start. I knew I had to make the effort, so I gulped and began. "Jen, I'm so sorry."

I halted to blink away tears. I felt truly ashamed. Jennifer threw her arm around me and laid her head on my shoulder. I now had the courage to go on. I told her everything — how Andrew Smith traded drugs with the Boss, how they blackmailed me into letting them use the storeroom of the museum for their weekend drop-offs. I told her about my suspicions concerning the involvement of Andrew and the White Boys in the fire at Granddad's farm. Jennifer listened to all of it without interrupting.

"What now, Jason?" she asked when I finished.

I shrugged. "I don't know. For now, maybe nothing at all."

"Nothing!" Jennifer cried, halting in her tracks. Then she noticed my furrowed brow. "Sorry, Jase! If we're to trust each other again, I guess I'll have to go along with you for the moment."

"Thanks, Stilts."

I smiled, and Jennifer giggled as she punched me playfully on the arm. We continued on our way home, exchanging idle banter about school and teachers — just like old times. As we rounded the corner of our street, we both saw Dad's car in the driveway.

"Granddad's home!" we both cried.

Jennifer and I raced to the front door. This time I opened it for my sister and followed her.

"Hello!" Jennifer called. "Anyone home?"

I hung up my coat and placed my books on the old radiator by the door. I had made my peace with Jennifer, but doing the same with Mom and Dad was going to be more difficult. I decided the best way was to say nothing, while improving my actions.

"In here!"

We both followed Mom's voice into the dining room, which now resembled a hospital room. Granddad rested on two large pillows in a reclining bed. He could easily reach metal trays laden with snack foods, drinks, and medicines. His face sported a plastic oxygen mask.

"Hi, Granddad!" I greeted.

Jennifer leaned over the bed railing and kissed him on the cheek. Granddad blustered, but smiled nevertheless.

"Hey!" Dad said as he, too, came into the room from the kitchen carrying a cup of tea. "That's the first smile I've seen from him in a couple of days. Nice going, Jen!"

We all laughed, and Granddad muttered, "Get this foul mask off me. There's nothing to smile about with this thing on my mug."

"Be nice, you old grouch," Grandma scolded as she gently lifted the mask and fondly smoothed Granddad's ruffled hair. "Besides, it's time for your rest. Take these pills and sleep."

"I don't want pills. Where's my medicine?"

"Doctor's orders, Dad," my father said. "Alcohol and painkillers don't mix. No more brandy for now."

Granddad scowled, but swallowed his pills with apple

juice. Then he settled back, and soon his eyes drooped. We all tiptoed out of the room. Grandma sat beside his bed and hummed a lovely church hymn while gently wiping perspiration from his forehead.

"How is he, Dad?" I asked.

"He'll be just fine, son."

I heard the tiredness in his voice.

Mom continued for him. "Jason, your grandfather's very tired. There are no broken bones, but there's some bad bruising and strained muscles. The pills will make him drowsy for the next few days. His lungs were badly inflamed with smoke, and he needs some enriched oxygen. For now he needs rest and lots of it. Your dad's right, though. He'll be just fine."

I left Mom, Dad, and Jennifer talking in the kitchen. I needed to be alone. Jennifer smiled at me as I left. It was a good feeling to know that my sister trusted me again.

I climbed the attic stairs, ignoring the dark shadows and the cold. Opening the door, I flopped onto my bed and stared at the ceiling. A ragged piece of wallpaper dangled within arm's reach above my head. I had noticed it before but had ignored it. Now I picked at the corner and peeled away long strips of brittle wall covering. Then I stopped. Kneeling, I peered more closely at the exposed wall. It looked as if an old newspaper were stuck there.

I ripped the rest of the wallpaper away and discovered that the newspaper plugged an old hole in the lathing. Pulling at one corner, I eased the yellowed newsprint from its cubbyhole. The paper crinkled and tore as I tugged it out. Finally, I managed to get the top portion free, then smoothed the wrinkles so I could read the headline from the old *Toronto Globe* newspaper: FEBRUARY 5, 1880. HORRIBLE TRAGEDY AT

LUCAN. FIVE PERSONS MURDERED BY MOB.

I read slowly over the creases and around the holes in the newspaper and soon realized this was an original report on the Donnelly murders in Lucan. It told of the barbaric attack on the Donnelly farmhouse, the brutal clubbing deaths of James, Johannah, and their son, Tom, and the death of their niece, Bridget. I read the names of the vigilantes, led by Constable James Carroll, who carried out the grisly deeds under the watch of ten-year-old Johnny O'Connor. After burning the Donnelly home, the vigilantes rode to Whalen's Corners. They wanted to kill William Donnelly, too, but instead shot his brother, John, to death as he came to answer the door. That night they murdered five people.

"Jason, are you there?"

I screamed.

I had concentrated so long on the newspaper article that I hadn't heard any approaching noises to my room.

"Stilts!" I yelled. "Call! Knock! Make noise, but don't sneak up on me."

Jennifer, rather than being annoyed, began to laugh.

"What's so funny?" I growled.

She giggled. "You are, silly!" She stooped to ease the pillow out of my hand and untangled me from the mass of covers I'd pulled off the bed. "Do you really think you could fight off anyone with this flimsy pillow?"

I squirmed impatiently under her helping hands and tripped again over the loose bedspread. I, too, had to laugh as I crashed again to the floor in a rumpled heap. After catching my breath, I handed the old paper to Jennifer.

"What's this?" she asked.

I said nothing, since she soon found the answer in the newspaper article.

"Where did you get this?"

"In that hole over there." I pointed at the torn wallpaper and the hole in the wall. Just then a numbing chill entered the room, and I saw white fog floating around my head with each breath I took. The mist streamed from Jennifer's mouth, too, as she gasped at the sudden drop in temperature. I wiped my face to rid the stickiness of what seemed like a large wet spiderweb. Then I saw it over Jennifer's shoulder. She must have felt something, too, or just followed my own stare.

"Jason!" she squealed.

"I know, Jen! I see him, too."

The bright globe of light came closer, and soon coalesced into a human shape — the moustached man dressed in a black frock coat. We clung to each other, paralyzed with fear. As the figure drew closer, he reached out a hand. His mouth moved as if he were speaking, but we only heard a continuous soft groaning that we couldn't understand. Then he stopped.

Pointing to the high vaulted ceiling of the attic, he traced bold red letters that spelled MURDERED! Dropping his arm, he turned back to Jen and me, trying once more to speak. Again there was the soft groan. But this time the light dimmed and the figure faded. Still we didn't move. Finally, Jennifer spoke. "Who or what was that?"

"It's him," I said.

"Him who?" she asked, her voice quavering.

"He's been here before," I explained. "He first came shortly after I moved into the attic. Then he appeared at the museum storeroom and left the same message. Granddad saw him, too!"

"Granddad?" Jennifer murmured.

"Yeah, it was midnight last Saturday night. Granddad

came to take me home from the museum. It was that same night, after he dropped me off, that the White Boys attacked his farm and he went to hospital."

Jennifer said nothing. I put my arms around her trembling shoulders. She shook from more than the cold, and I feared I had told her too much.

"Jason," she said meekly, "do you think that ghost is trying to tell us something?"

"He's trying to warn us about something — that's for sure," I said as I stared at the fading blood-red letters etched across the ceiling. I thought hard for several moments. "We need Granddad's help with this."

"But, Jason," Jennifer protested, "he's been through so much."

"And could go through a lot worse if we don't ask for his help. Besides, knowing Granddad, he'll be so grumpy after two days in that bed no one will be able to keep him still. If we get him involved in this, we might be doing Grandma a big favour."

I was right. After two days, Grandma found herself chasing Granddad down the main hall, through the living room, and back into the dining room where she cornered him by the large sideboard. Clutching him by the ear, she dragged him back to bed, ignoring his curses and threats. Once back in bed, Grandma reattached his oxygen mask. Granddad still breathed heavily even after the shortest of walks. She plugged in his IV with its mild dosage of muscle relaxants, and he soon calmed down.

After Grandma settled Granddad, she joined Mom, Jennifer, and me in the kitchen. "That man will be the death of me," she said. "He's too blasted stubborn."

"Now, Grandma," Mom cautioned, "it's just a sign that he's getting better. Each day he's stronger and is able to take longer walks. Soon you'll be back at the farm where he'll be able to get even more exercise. At least he'll be out of your way there. It's awfully cramped for you two in this house."

"Oh, Ellen," Grandma moaned, "I didn't mean to sound unappreciative. It's just that he worries me so. I do want him to get better, and I'm trying hard to be patient."

Jennifer moved to comfort Grandma when she saw her hands shake while lifting her teacup. I shook my head at her. I knew Jennifer's gesture would only embarrass Grandma. I nodded again, and we started to leave.

"Tell you what!" Mom said to Grandma. Jennifer and I stopped out of sight and listened. "Tom's off on assignment this afternoon and I'm free from shifts this weekend. Granddad's resting quietly now. Why don't you and I take a girls' afternoon off? We can go to lunch and then shop. London's only twenty minutes away."

"But, Ellen, what about Ted? I can't —"

Mom snorted. "Nonsense! He's sleeping and will be for the next two or three hours if I'm any judge of the amount of relaxant you gave him. It's ten o'clock. You go and rest for half an hour, then get ready. We can leave by 11:30 and be in London by noon. We'll be back by three or four at the latest."

"But he needs —"

"No buts!" Mom chided. "Jennifer and Jason are both home this afternoon. They can look after him."

Grandma giggled. "Thank you, Ellen. A girls' afternoon off sounds great. Besides, I need a spending spree. A few shopping bills will serve the old goat right."

Jennifer and I stifled our laughter as we sneaked away from the kitchen doorway.

Mom walked Grandma to the car at 11:30, just as she said she would. Jennifer and I listened patiently as Grandma went over Granddad's list of medications for the afternoon.

"No brandy!" she warned as she jabbed her tiny finger into my chest.

"No brandy, Grandma," Jennifer said for both of us. "We promise. Now go and spend a fortune. I want to see that pretty red blouse you've been eyeing at The Bay."

"That thing's too young for me," she sniffed. "But it would sure be fun. I'll buy it!"

We all chuckled.

When they left, Jennifer checked on Granddad. His head was slumped sideways, his eyes were closed, and he was snoring. "He'll sleep for at least another hour." Jennifer closed the sliding door between the living and dining rooms, then walked over to the television and turned it off.

"Hey!" I yelled. "Tiger Woods was about to sink that birdie for the lead. He's tied at ten under."

"And you're ten under your best grade average. We have a biology test on Monday. Study!"

I scowled and almost retorted with one of my "Stilts" insults, but this was a new Jason. I didn't want to be angry with anyone, especially Jennifer. "Yeah, you're right," I said, pouting. "Besides, I have to work at the museum after closing again tonight."

Both of us headed up to our rooms, but I decided to use the desk in Mom and Dad's room. I had missed some test notes, and it was easier to study with Jennifer near. Once settled, I found the studying went quite well. Only the occasional steaming ping from the radiators made me jump. I looked for my ghostly friend standing at the door, but he never showed.

After about an hour, Jennifer called, "Do you want anything from the kitchen, Jason?"

"Please, Jen, yes, burger, fries, and a shake to go!"

"Good luck," she said. "What do you really want?"

"A pop would be great, thanks."

I stood away from the desk, stretched my arms above my head, and arched my back. Gazing at my study notes, I felt proud of the amount of work I'd done in such a short time.

"Granddad!" Jennifer suddenly shouted. "What are you doing out of bed?"

I stopped my self-congratulations and rushed down the stairs, where I met Jennifer and Granddad heading into the dining room from the kitchen.

"But it's my medicine time," Granddad whined. "The doctor said I could have a small snifter after my nap."

"He said no such thing, and you know it!" Jennifer said, trying to sound stern, but only managing to giggle.

"Can I help?" I asked.

"Sure! Take Granddad back to the dining room and help him with his slippers and housecoat. He can sit up in the living room and watch the end of the golf game with you. I'll make tea and cut some of Grandma's chocolate cake. I might just pour an extra bit of brandy over your piece if you're good, Granddad."

He chuckled. "That's my girl!"

I helped Granddad to his easy chair in front of the television, then all three of us sat in comfortable silence. Even Jennifer showed some excitement at the pitching tricks Woods used from the sand traps. Granddad snarled at Mike Weir for a missed putt and asked for a second piece of cake. Jennifer obliged with another, smaller dash of brandy. At the end of the broadcast I turned off the television.

"Hey!" Granddad protested.

"Easy, Granddad," I soothed. "Jennifer and I want to talk to you."

"What have you two been up to that I should know about?"

I ignored Jennifer's warning glare. "We saw him again today."

"Who?" Granddad asked. "Where?" Then he realized what I was talking about. "Not in this house, too?"

"Here!" I said. "In the attic, and Jennifer saw him, too. The same one as at the museum."

"Tell me what happened!" Granddad demanded.

Both Jennifer and I relaxed when we saw the old twinkle come back into his eyes. Slowly, he dragged his finger around his cake plate to wipe up the rest of the brandy and waited for us to continue. Our nervousness lessened as we realized that our story only served to perk Granddad up rather than upset him.

I explained about the old newspaper I'd found under the wallpaper in my room, the immediate reappearance of the ghost, and his attempt to talk to us. Granddad wanted to see the spot where the apparition had written MURDERED on the ceiling, but Jennifer firmly said no to that idea. Granddad let us finish our story.

"Why is he here?" I asked.

"I'm not sure exactly, son. I don't think he means any harm. It's not often that a ghost speaks, and I think the sign is a friendly warning — not to harm us but to warn us."

"Andrew Smith," I whispered.

"Who?" Granddad demanded. But he didn't wait for my answer and continued with his own theory. "The ghost is probably what we call a 'forerunner.'"

"Forerunner?" Jennifer echoed.

"A forerunner," Granddad said, "is a spiritual being who's trying to warn us of some harm that might occur. He or she is usually drawn back to this physical world by a familiar object, and visits only those places where those objects might be found."

"Such as the artifacts at the museum," I suggested.

"And the newspaper in the attic!" Jennifer gasped.

"Exactly!" Granddad said. "That's why Rob Salts may have so many spirits appearing around his place. It's full of antiques and old buildings. The house he lives in is the same one William Donnelly rebuilt on his parents' property after the massacre."

"I never knew any of this," I said.

Granddad paused.

"Go on, Granddad," I urged.

"Sorry, Jason," he said, "but that ghost you described sure sounds familiar. He reminds me of a photo of one of the Feeheleys — was it James or William?" He coughed heavily and stopped to catch his breath. Jennifer and I realized he was tiring, but also knew he wanted to continue his story.

"I did read in Ray Fazakas's book *The Donnelly Album* that James, on a number of occasions, nearly confessed his part in the raid that night and seems to be the one most remorseful for it all. He was, after all, a good friend of the Donnellys."

"But why betray them?" I asked.

"I think the Feeheley brothers may have been bribed. It seems their father had an outstanding mortgage on his farm of five hundred dollars that would be paid if his sons helped set up the raid for that February night. If that's the case, maybe this ghost is one of the Feeheleys wanting to make a final confession or give a warning of things to come."

"Such as barn burnings?" I mused thoughtfully.

"You may be right, Jason," Granddad said. "And there may be more to come."

Chapter 10

Jennifer helped Granddad back to bed, where he soon fell asleep. I tramped up the stairs to collect my books and get ready for my museum shift. I had just finished a light supper when Mom and Grandma arrived home.

"Hi! Bye!" I said.

I leaned over, kissed Grandma lightly on the cheek, and hugged Mom. Then I stepped back to see the shocked expression on her face. I hadn't hugged her like that in a long time. We both smiled at each other.

"Are you dressed well?" Mom asked. "It's cold. Be careful out there."

Usually, I rudely shrugged off any sign of affection, but times were different now. I paused at the open door. "Thanks, Mom!" I smiled again as I closed the door.

Upon reaching the street, I looked back through the large picture window of the living room and chuckled as I watched Grandma unwrap the tissue paper from her new purchases. She held up a bright red blouse — the one Jennifer had said she should buy from The Bay. All three laughed as Grandma did a mock modelling act with her new clothes. I walked to the end of the street, feeling warmer than I had in a long time. Things were going to be different.

The night closing at the museum went smoothly. I mopped the floors, emptied the trash, turned off the lights, and shut down the computers. When I shifted the last bolt to lock the front door, I heard a faint tapping at the back. It was the signal. The miniature pendulum clock struck twelve.

"Andrew Smith!" I muttered.

I didn't hurry to the back door. When I finally opened it, Andrew brushed me aside to get out of the biting cold.

"What took you so long?" he demanded. "It's cold out there, you know."

"Not cold enough to burn barns and send old men to the hospital, though, is it?"

I jumped as Andrew swivelled toward me. "I told you I had nothing to do with that." He grabbed my shirt collar and pinned me to the wall, knocking over a bucket and some mops. We both stopped struggling when we saw the blue and white lights flash in the alley.

"Constable Howard, I'll bet," Andrew said. "You'd better hope he doesn't come in!"

I didn't argue with him. The last thing I wanted was a visit from the constable.

The car stopped, and a large white beam from a searchlight streamed through the tiny upper window of the storeroom. Andrew and I crouched against the wall below the window and let the beam move around the room. Then it was shut off. We both breathed more easily when we heard the car door slam. The cruiser's lights flicked off, and tires crunched in the snow as the vehicle moved down the alley to the main street.

"I'm out of here!" Andrew snarled. "The Boss won't like you snitching to the cops, Stevens."

"But I didn't know —" The door slammed in my face before I could finish. I straightened the overturned bucket and mops, grabbed my coat, and locked the back door. Trudging through the thin layer of freshly fallen snow, I pulled my collar around my neck and ears and ducked my head against the mounting wind.

I didn't see the car following me down the alley, so I jumped when I heard the light beep of a horn. Blinking into the blinding headlights, I hopped to the side of the road and waited for the car to pass. It was an OPP cruiser. It stopped beside me, and the driver's window rolled down. "Need a lift, Jason?"

"Constable Howard!" I cried.

Just when I thought everything was getting better, it was slowly getting worse. Realizing I had little choice, I mumbled a weak thanks, walked around to the passenger side of the cruiser, and climbed in.

I fumbled with the seat belt, then slumped against the door. Constable Howard said nothing, so I stared out of the frosted window at the dimly lit Lucan streets. At the end of the alley the constable turned right instead of left. I sat up and looked at him, knowing we were going the wrong way.

"I need to check out a crime scene from earlier this evening," he said. "I hope you don't mind."

I shrugged. As if I had a choice, I thought to myself, squirming in the seat and pulling at the seat belt. I was uncomfortable and just wanted to go home. I became even more puzzled as the cruiser drifted to the outskirts of town and headed toward London. About a mile outside town Constable Howard engaged his turn signal at the corner of the Roman Line. Large searchlights buried in the snow shone brightly on the tall steeple of St. Patrick's Roman Catholic Church.

"The Donnellys are buried there," Constable Howard said. "But I guess you know that already."

I said nothing, but Constable Howard continued after

a short pause. "An old superstition says that if you leave a coin on the top of a gravestone, it will ward off evil spirits. The cemetery caretaker often collects the money and puts it in the alms box at the front door of the church. He didn't collect much money this past summer and fall."

Constable Howard didn't wait for any response from me, but kept talking. "Could be it's the cold weather and not many people are coming to the cemetery. But the caretaker did notice that the Donnelly tombstone had been vandalized. Several large chips are missing."

Still I said nothing, but I grew more anxious. Why the roundabout car ride and the history lecture? Was he trying to draw me out?

"The original Donnelly tombstone was removed in 1964. The Lucan people were really sensitive about the Donnelly murders even after almost a hundred years, and they objected to the word MURDERED on the stone."

I shuddered when I heard that word.

"Sorry, Jason. Have I kept the heat down too low?"

"No, I'm fine, thanks. Maybe I should be getting home. My folks get worried when it's this late."

"Yes, I guess you're right. But my first stop's right here."

Constable Howard turned the cruiser into the freshly ploughed parking lot. "Did you know that the original Donnelly tombstone is in the possession of the Donnelly family members? A retired World War II air force tail gunner named Bill Lord inherited it from his mother, Nora."

"I never knew that."

"Coming?" he asked.

I took my time unhooking my seat belt. I didn't trust Constable Howard's reasons for taking me with him.

"It seems that the museum committee, with support from the mayor, would like to have the tombstone for display. They feel it's time to recognize the Donnellys and their place in Lucan's history. Quite a change in public opinion, don't you think?"

Dad had told me that the people of Lucan refused to talk about those dark times in the 1870s and 1880s when terror struck the district. "Do you think they'll get it?" I asked.

"Not likely," Constable Howard said. "Old Mrs. Lord left strict instructions for that tombstone not to be put on display. Her son seems to be following her wishes."

We arrived at the vestry door, and Constable Howard stopped. He flicked on his flashlight and passed its powerful beam over the outer rim of the door, halting at the tarnished lock. The beam picked up scratches and deep gouges on the wood frame.

"What happened?" I asked.

"Break-and-enter," Constable Howard said. "The alms box in the church by the altar was robbed. I guess if people can't steal coins from tombstones, they'll try somewhere else. I just need to get pictures with my night film of footprints around the door. Wait here, Jason."

The constable ducked under the yellow police surveillance tape that surrounded the entranceway and left me to my own thoughts. Not the White Boys again, surely? Stealing money from a church? Then I remembered that they hadn't shown up for their usual pickup at the museum tonight, and Andrew hadn't stayed around long after Constable Howard had left the first time. Barn burning? Church robbery? What was next?

"I'm finished here, Jason. Next stop, the Salts farm."

Wearily, I climbed back into the cruiser. Constable

Howard reversed the car out of the church lot and headed up the Roman Line. Gone were the bright lights of the village streets. The cruiser's high beams shone brightly into the cold night. Only a few flickering farm lights dotted the darkness.

Pointing to one set of lights, Constable Howard showed me the Salts farm. "That's the old Donnelly farm where it all started and ended so many years ago. James and Johannah were scheduled to appear in court on February 4, 1880, on charges of theft of farm equipment. Very early that morning the vigilantes arrived. Constable James Carroll entered the house and handcuffed Tom on an unknown arrest warrant. The rest, shall we say, is history. Later in 1880, William built the frame house you see now. He planted five chestnut trees on the front lawn, one for each murdered family member. The homestead stayed in the Donnelly family until 1939 when it was sold. There were no more Donnelly male heirs after that time."

"So Granddad was right," I muttered.

"Right about what?" Constable Howard asked.

What could I tell him? About the ghost at home and the museum? I hesitated for the longest time, then said, "Just that spiritual forces are attracted to old places and things. He thinks that's why Mr. Salts has so many ghosts at his place."

Constable Howard chuckled. "Never thought of it that way before. Then again, I always thought of them as just stories. I'm not a real believer, I guess."

I said no more. We didn't turn into the Saltses' driveway but continued up the road. Turning on his caution lights, the constable pulled onto the narrow shoulder. As he opened the door of the cruiser, he said, "Last stop. Won't be a minute." He collected his flashlight and camera. "I need a few more nighttime shots."

Not wanting to stay in the cruiser by myself, I followed him across an old culvert and avoided the thigh-deep snow in the ditch. We passed through an opening in the fence that looked like an old gate. The wind had been strong for the past few days and still rattled the bare branches of the old maples along the line. Constable Howard flashed his beam across a low stone wall — no more than thirty centimetres high.

"Know what that is?" he asked.

I shook my head and huddled more deeply into my parka.

"That's what's left of the old Donnelly schoolhouse. In order to show some goodwill toward the community, Old Jim Donnelly donated this land to the local trustees for a schoolhouse. The villagers built it in the 1860s and used it until the Cedar Swamp Schoolhouse opened in 1874. Jim was serving his life sentence for the murder of Pat Farrell in Kingston Penitentiary and hoped his gift would make amends to the community."

I kicked at the small snowdrifts that banked the foundation. "What's that fireplace doing here?"

Constable Howard flashed his light over to the firepit. "Mr. Salts has seen the local kids stop here on weekend nights, especially in the summer. They light small fires and hang out. He doesn't mind too much as long as they control the fires and don't bring beer or drugs onto the property. He's had no trouble until now." Constable Howard directed his light off to the right.

I saw square black shapes mounted on crude wooden platforms. The platforms lay upside down, and their legs stuck up into the night sky. "What happened?" I asked.

"More night visitors. Mr. Salts phoned me last night to report a fire at the schoolhouse site. It was the first he'd seen at this time of year, and he thought something was suspicious, so he called me."

"What are those crates over there?"

"Mr. Salts's beehives. He's a beekeeper and makes the best natural honey I've ever tasted. When he came out to investigate the fire, he heard shouts and laughter. By the time he pulled up and got out of his car, he was unable to stop the culprits. They sped off in a dark red Dodge Ram. He didn't follow it. That's when he discovered his overturned beehives. I was hoping to take one more set of photos of tracks around the scene, but the wind has swept them clean. Ready for home?"

"Yes, thanks." I shivered from more than just the cold. The violence of the Donnelly years seemed to be coming back. A nauseating feeling flooded my stomach. I had strong suspicions who might be responsible, and I knew I had the power to help stop it. But at what cost?

Again I slid close to the passenger door and hid my face inside my parka. Constable Howard and I said nothing for a long while. He answered his dispatcher to forward his location, then drove silently through the town.

I gasped when I saw the grey Cadillac limousine pass us going south — in the same direction we had just come from! Both of us followed it past the window of the cruiser, and Constable Howard still watched its progress through his rearview mirror.

"Have you seen that Caddie around much lately, Jason?"

"Some," I mumbled. "Not much. Do you know anything about it?"

"I was hoping you would. The most common sighting is at your school at the end of the day. One guy you know,

Andrew Smith, usually hangs around the Caddie, right?"

"Beats me," I whispered.

I stared out the passenger window so Constable Howard couldn't see the sheer panic on my face. I hoped he'd let the subject drop, but he didn't.

"I can't prove it yet, but I suspect Smith is behind the drug dealing with the kids at school. The evidence is building quite quickly against him as well as against the one they call J.T., the hippie who's always riding around in the Caddie. But I'd really like to catch the man they call the Boss in the act. Without that I can't touch him."

"You could arrest Smith and J.T., couldn't you?" I asked.

"You're right, but I could probably catch those two anytime I wanted. I need the big guy in the operation, and that's the Boss."

"So you're planning on using the other two as bait?"

"That or until someone else comes forward with other information. I hope I don't have to wait much longer. I don't like to see those drugs on the streets."

Constable Howard took his eyes off the road and studied me. I jerked away and counted the street corners to my turn. Finally, he turned down my street and into my driveway. I fumbled with the seat belt and grabbed at the stiff door handle.

"Here, let me get that," he said. "I've been meaning to have that handle replaced, but I never have enough time. Don't worry about your folks, Jason. They knew you're with me."

"Thanks," I said, wondering what that meant.

I pushed open the door and had one foot on the ground when Constable Howard spoke to me again. "See you on Thursday — same time and place, Jason. And if you have any leads or anything you want to talk to me about, let me know. Say hello to your folks for me. I hope your grandfather's feeling better."

I had no time to wave good night. When Constable Howard reversed out the driveway, he flashed his overhead cruiser lights, blared his siren, and skidded through the slush as he sped toward the main street.

Chapter 11

I ran up the front steps two at time, then jumped back as Jennifer opened the door.

"Geez, Stilts!" I cried. Quickly, I tried to recover, then saw an angry blush creep over her face at my use of the old nickname. "Where's Mom and Dad?"

"Out! Dinner and a movie!" she said tersely as she firmly shut the front door behind us.

"Look, Jen," I said, "I really am sorry. I didn't expect you and you did scare me."

Jennifer giggled. "The look on your face made me think you'd seen a ghost."

"Ghost? Jen, have you seen another ghost?" I looked at her in panic.

"Easy, Jason," she said. "Grandma's asleep upstairs, and Granddad was pretty restless about a half-hour ago, so I came down to make him some warm milk. I showed him the old *Globe* newspaper, and we talked about the ghost we saw. That's all. Want some hot chocolate? Water's still warm."

"Sure, thanks," I murmured.

I wandered into the living room and said hello to Granddad, who was rereading the *Globe* article and sipping steaming milk. I sniffed a faint tinge of brandy and smiled, then slumped into the overstuffed recliner by the fireplace. Jennifer came back with my hot chocolate.

After a few moments, I finally said to Jennifer, "I think it's time."

"Time?" Granddad piped up. "Time for what?"

"Granddad," I began, "I'm in big trouble and I need help."

I told my story to him. At first he seemed too shocked to answer. Then I saw him become more relaxed, and he settled back into the rocker with the cup of warm milk.

I explained Andrew Smith's midnight visits to the museum. Granddad's eyebrows twitched slightly when I told him about the drugs Smith sold there. Still he didn't interrupt. I saw his jaw clench when I outlined my suspicions about who burnt his barn. Finally, I told him about my visits to Constable Howard's crime scenes at the church and the Salts farm.

"Darn it, boy!" Granddad blustered. "Did you tell Howard about all this?"

"I'm going to tomorrow," I said.

Granddad shivered. All these revelations were a bit too much for him.

"Come on, Granddad, I think it's time for bed," Jennifer said. She wrapped his housecoat around his shoulders, and we both guided him back to his hospital bed. He let us tuck his blankets around him and was snoring peacefully when Jennifer leaned over to kiss his cheek. I turned out the living-room lights and followed my sister up the stairs and to sleep.

When I tumbled out of bed the next morning, I was tangled in sheets and my T-shirt and shorts were stuck to my body like wet towels. Too frustrated to get my sodden hair to lie properly, I pulled on a dirty pair of jeans and a faded sweatshirt, then slowly trudged down the stairs and through the hallway to the kitchen to begin my confessions.

Mom and Dad were my first challenge of the day; Constable Howard would be next. The prospect weighed heavily on me, and even the aroma of fresh bacon and the sound of sizzling French toast — my favourite breakfast — didn't improve my mood.

"Good morning, Jas —" Grandma stopped in mid-sentence. "You look awful, Jason! Are you sick?" She put her hand on my forehead. "Ellen, the boy's hot and he's sweating. Does he have the flu?"

Mom checked my forehead and peered into my eyes. Dad stood at her shoulder. "You look like someone took a baseball bat to your face, son. Your eyes are two large black holes. What do you think, Ellen?"

"I'm not sick!" I shot back. When I saw my parents flinch, I quickly said, "Sorry, it's just that —" I couldn't go on any further. I bowed my head and leaned against the counter.

Jennifer put her arm around my shoulder, and I heard Granddad shuffle into the kitchen. There were none of his usual grumpy complaints, and he, too, stood beside me.

"Go for it, son," he encouraged me. "It'll be all right."

I straightened and again began my story. I had to gulp back the tears a few times as Mom's loud sobs and Grandma's shocked gasps unfolded with my story. When I finished, no one said a word. Dad looked directly into my eyes. His stare remained blank.

"I need to call Constable Howard," I said. "Could I have his phone number, please?"

"I'll call for you," Dad said. He strode across the kitchen floor on his way to the living room and the telephone. "Granddad's right, Jason. Everything will be all right."

Mom wiggled between Jennifer and me to hug me closely to her tear-stained face. "It's not just your fault. It's ours, too. What with the court case, the move, new jobs, and Granddad's illness, we haven't had enough time for you kids. I'm so sorry."

I couldn't contain myself any longer and collapsed in heaving sobs into Mom's arms. She sat me down at the kitchen table and gave me some water. By the time Dad returned to the room, I had pulled myself together.

"Constable Howard will be here in a half-hour," Dad said. He sat down at the table beside me. "You know, Jason, Doug and I have suspected something like this for several weeks now."

"Tom!" Mom cried.

"Easy, Ellen," my father said. "Between Dad, me, and Doug, we've kept a close eye on Jason to be sure no harm came to him."

"That's why Constable Howard came cruising by so often," I said. "And, Granddad, you were around the museum after hours a lot of the time, weren't you?"

"And I've been investigating the White Boys almost since we came to Lucan," Dad said. "We didn't know all the details — at least until now. It took a lot of courage for you to tell us, Jason."

"Why didn't you tell *me*?" Mom demanded. Anger still flashed in her eyes.

"There was nothing to tell," Dad insisted, trying to defend himself. "Jason wasn't into or dealing drugs. His grades at school were improving, and Mr. Simpson had no complaints about our son's behaviour or class attendance at school. As I said, he wasn't doing anything really wrong. And if it looked as if he was going to get into trouble, there were four of us to protect him."

"Four?" I looked up at Dad in surprise. "You, Granddad, Constable Howard … Who's the fourth?"

"Andrew Smith," Dad said. "Originally, Andrew lived with his folks in Clinton. He finished high school and needed a job or some direction in his life. He came to Lucan to live with his grandparents for a short while. Then he went away to college — two years of training at OPP Headquarters. He showed an interest and aptitude for undercover surveillance. When the drug problems and thefts broke out in this area, the OPP transferred Andrew to Lucan on special assignment. He's been working with Constable Howard ever since."

"Wow!" I gasped. "I never would have guessed. I knew he seemed a little older, but he still fit right in with the rest of us."

"He's twenty-one," Dad said, "and just out of police training. He almost didn't get the assignment, but since he knew Lucan, is only a few years older than the seniors at the school, and looks younger than his age, we decided to take a chance."

"Yeah," Jennifer said, "he's cute!"

"Jennifer!" I scolded.

She blushed, and I laughed. Then the doorbell rang.

"That's Doug now," Dad said. "Want me to get it, Ellen?"

"No!" Mom snapped. "I have a few words to say to little Dougie Howard." She went off to "greet" the constable.

None of us moved. We cringed at the sharp whispers we heard from the hall. It didn't sound as if Constable Howard had much chance to say anything. When the two walked into the kitchen, Mom looked flushed, but the anger in her eyes had disappeared. Constable Howard seemed sheepish.

He quietly took a seat and readily accepted a cup of coffee from Mom.

After a long silence, I nervously asked, "What now?"

Constable Howard looked first at Dad, then at Mom. "We continue just as before."

"What?" Mom said. "Didn't you listen to what I had to say, Mr. Howard?"

"Yes, I did," Constable Howard said, "but technically Jason has violated his parole by associating with suspected criminals and dealing in drugs. If you're willing to follow my plan, I'll cut him free."

"How do you expect to do that?" Mom demanded. I knew she still wasn't convinced.

"I can plead that Jason was working with me all along on this drug surveillance. As his special parole officer, I can claim I knew all about his actions and that he was under constant police supervision."

Mom calmed down a little. I put my hand over her clenched fist, and Dad rubbed her sagging shoulders. After gently patting her, he left the kitchen.

"It'll be okay, Mom," Jennifer said.

"We have the advantage now, Ellen," Dad added after he returned. "Jason will have even more complete police undercover protection than before. That is if he's willing …"

I needed no more encouragement. I had to make things right for my family and myself. "Yes!" I cried.

"Good!" Constable Howard said. "Andrew here, Tom?"

"Yes, he is," Dad said. "I went to the car to get him. Andrew, come in, please."

Andrew Smith still wore his gleaming studded leather jacket with its upturned collar. His baggy sweatshirt and the tails of his shirt hung over his belt line, which rested on his hips. His jeans bagged at the knees, and the upturned cuffs dragged on the floor. His white-laced boots stayed at the door, and he stood in white athletic socks.

"Mrs. Stevens, my name's Andrew Smith. It's a pleasure to meet you, and I *will* look after your son for you."

Mom stared at him but didn't speak.

"Sit down, Andrew," Constable Howard said. "We need to do some planning, and it's best the family hears this."

"Yes, sir," Andrew said. "First, we'll soon need a new place to do our business. Jason's thirty hours of community service at the museum will be over in another two weeks. I found out that it was the White Boys who set that fire in the Cedar Swamp Schoolhouse. They used it as a regular meeting place until Jason came along." He gently punched my shoulder and grinned.

I had trouble getting over my initial shock at Andrew's real identity and had difficulty speaking. "If that's the case, how am I going to continue to be involved?"

"Good question," Andrew said. "I'll still be putting pressure on you to help me distribute drugs, but only this time in an expanded operation at the school."

"No, Tom!" Mom cried. "I won't have it!"

"But, Mom," I protested.

"Ellen, let Andrew finish," Dad said. "It's not dangerous and it's quite safe."

"Mrs. Stevens," Andrew assured Mom, "Jason won't be selling drugs at school. It won't come to that, and the dealers will be arrested first. But I may need Jennifer's help, too."

Mom's face blanched, and her hands began to shake. Andrew continued quickly before she could interrupt him. "I've set the stage. I threatened Jason that I'd involve Jennifer if he didn't cooperate fully. It seems my buyers suspect the drugs I've been dealing them aren't genuine."

"How did that happen?" I asked.

"Easy enough," Andrew said. "When I picked up the night's batch from J.T., I always had time to get it over to the office and substitute it with Old Dutch pipe tobacco. They were often drunk on liquor and didn't notice the difference. It was risky at times, but it's worked so far."

"But if your buyers are suspicious, how do you plan to handle that?" Dad asked.

"The Boss has already heard the rumours of the petty theft and property damage. He isn't too pleased. It threatens exposure of his drug trade. I'll try to persuade him to meet the buyers and me at the old schoolhouse next Saturday night. To show good faith, I'll ask him to bring a fresh drug shipment straight from Colombia for the boys to test and buy. I need to protect my cover a little longer. If I bring Jason and Jennifer along as my new 'druggies,' I can use them as a sign of good faith with the Boss that I'm still loyal."

"How does this all end?" Mom groaned. "First Jason and now Jennifer?"

"It ends that night, Ellen," Constable Howard said, jumping into the conversation as he moved to Mom's side. "The problem we've had is catching the Boss in the act of an actual sale of drugs. Andrew's collected enough evidence to convict J.T. If we promise the White Boys a plea bargain because they haven't really been dealing in illegal drugs, we can nail him for sure. The Boss produces his new drugs that night and makes the sale directly to Andrew, then we have him. An OPP drug squad will be hidden at the scene and will move in once they're signalled."

Mom's face was even paler now. She sat listlessly, not saying a word. Constable Howard moved closer and gripped her hands. "I know I'm asking a lot, Ellen. I'm calling on our old friendship, hoping you'll trust me that nothing will happen to your kids."

Still no answer.

"If either you, Tom, or the kids say no," Constable Howard continued, "we stop now. No more, I promise. But this is the best chance we have to stop the violence and the drugs around here."

Mom finally nodded, then sobbed. Jennifer and I rushed to kneel by her side. I heard Jennifer whisper, "Thanks, Mom. This is important."

Chapter 12

On the following Saturday night I arrived early at the museum and helped Granddad close up the front. As he reached to turn out the porch lights, I saw him lean against the front desk.

"You all right, Granddad?" I asked.

He and Grandma were staying with us for another week. The hospital bed had been taken away two days ago, along with the IV stands and oxygen tanks. The doctor had been encouraging Granddad to get as much exercise as he could but not to overdo it.

We all expected him to be overeager to get back to normal. He soon realized, though, that he was still weak, so he didn't complain when we ordered him to sit in his rocker and rest. A walk in the brisk sunshine earlier this afternoon had helped, but now at 5:30 he was tired.

"I'm fine, Jason," he said a little too briskly. "Thanks for asking. I'm just a little short of breath. The doctor told me to expect that."

A horn sounded in the front parking lot. We peered out and saw Dad's car idling by the front steps. Granddad waved to show he was getting ready. Dad waved back and stayed in the car. He knew he had to let Granddad do as much for himself as possible. I hefted his coat over his shoulders, then handed him his hat and scarf. He slipped into his fleece-lined boots and headed toward the door, then stopped.

"Good luck tonight, Jason. If you run into trouble, give me a call."

I smiled. "Sure thing, Granddad! Andrew should be here soon. Now that I know who he is, I feel much safer."

"He sure had us all fooled," Granddad said. "I hope he can pull this off one more time. Say hello to Finnegan!"

I laughed at the nickname Jennifer, Granddad, and I had given our spiritual visitor. I followed Granddad to the porch and waited until he took the steps one at a time and climbed into the car. Dad beeped the horn again as he drove down the alley toward the main street.

I had no sooner locked the front door when I heard the coded taps at the back. I dodged the artifact displays and hurried to answer. "Andrew!" I panted. "Come in!"

Andrew quickly closed the door behind him. "Your grandfather just left?"

I nodded. "No one else has come. I sure hope Finnegan doesn't pay us a visit tonight."

Andrew half smiled and glanced at me out of the corner of his eye. I knew he didn't buy into all this spirituality, but he willingly accepted our points of view. He often suggested a staged ghostly event as a distraction when we finally confronted the Boss. Jennifer and I humoured Andrew as much as he indulged us. We told him we'd call Finnegan any time he needed him.

"You're right," Andrew said. "Yet I'd like to see their faces if and when your Finnegan ever does show up!" We both laughed.

Then Andrew signalled for quiet. I heard the faint voices grow stronger as some of the White Boys tried to out-argue and out-shout each other.

"Stupid!" Andrew said, shaking his head. "They're

drunk again! No wonder Doug Howard was able to pick up on these guys so quickly." He shook his head even more vigorously when the arranged light taps turned into echoing thuds on the door.

"Come on!" one of the White Boys shouted. "Open up, Smith! It's cold out here!"

Andrew breathed deeply, reached for the door, and jerked it open. One of the boys staggered into him, and the rest giggled at their tottering friend. A sweet smell drifted in with their misty breath.

"Welcome, Tyler!" Andrew snarled. "You guys have been drinking again! The Boss doesn't like that. It draws more public attention than he likes."

The rest of the gang pushed by Andrew as they hurried in from the cold.

Tyler jostled me against the back wall. "Move out of the way, Stevens!" he ordered, trying to regain his composure after his clumsy entrance. He gripped my shirt and slammed me into the broom rack, but I let him bully me. Then he stepped up toe to toe with Andrew and breathed sickly fumes into his face. "If the Boss wants us to behave, he'd better get us some proper dope. Those flakes you've been selling us are junk."

"So I've been told," Andrew said as he pushed Tyler away. "I already spoke to the Boss, and he agreed to bring a fresh batch of Colombia's finest and personally deliver it to you."

"When and where?"

"Not here!" Andrew said. "Not anymore!"

"Why not?" Tyler demanded.

"Jason finishes his community service tonight and won't be back. Besides, Howard checks this place out almost every weekend. It's too well-known."

"You snitching on us, Stevens?" Tyler croaked. He made a move toward me, but Andrew blocked his way and held a firm grip on his clenched fist, so he stepped back. "How do we know he won't snitch to Howard?"

"No worries!" Andrew said. "I showed Jason how easy it would be to plant stuff in his sister's locker one day last week. He nearly wet his pants on the spot." Andrew laughed and nudged Tyler, who joined him. "Yeah, Jason will behave. After this, both he and his sister will gladly help us run our drugs — free of charge! Right, Jason?" Andrew gently tapped my face in mock slaps.

"No screw-ups, Stevens," Tyler added as he jabbed a finger into my chest. "Your sister is a sweet kid, and I wouldn't want anything to happen to her."

"You wouldn't dare!" I growled, lunging at Tyler. This time Andrew blocked my way and shoved me back into the broom racks. The rest of the gang laughed at me again.

"Right then!" Andrew said. "The next drop will be one week from tonight. We meet at the Cedar Swamp Schoolhouse at midnight. The Boss and J.T. will both be there with the new stuff. I'm sure you know how to get in."

"This new stuff better be good. If not, a raid on the Salts farm will give the Boss more attention than he ever dreamed of. Besides, that ghostbuster needs a lesson or two. He should stop telling those ghost stories of his. He might get the same treatment as those Donnellys way back when."

Tyler and the other White Boys left. Andrew stayed for a few moments while I tidied the storeroom and locked the back door.

"There," Andrew said, "that was easy enough. The Boss is so angry with these twerps that he hasn't grown suspicious."

"How did you convince him it wasn't you who was

giving out the tobacco?"

Andrew laughed. "I didn't have to. When the Boss heard about the liquor store break-in and their other shenanigans, he thought they were trying to muscle into his territory. He thinks they're into bootlegging liquor and are reselling his drugs in smaller packages at the same price. He doesn't believe their story about poor-quality stuff."

"Then why would the Boss agree to meet with them and offer them a better grade of drugs?"

Andrew shrugged. "One way to lure them into a meeting and teach them a lesson, I guess. Anyway, the trap is set for both the Boss and the White Boys. We'll let Doug know that all went well tonight, so we can finalize our plans for next Saturday."

For the rest of the week Jennifer and I tried to act normally, but it was hard to do. We constantly passed the White Boys in the school halls and ignored their threatening sneers. On the second day I saw Jennifer trapped between two of the White Boys, who pressed around her. I broke free of the crowd and pushed my way in front of Jennifer.

"What's up, Tyler?" I growled. "Leave her alone!"

"Look, punk," Tyler snarled, "this is the way it is. Smith said you guys were going to help sell the Boss's drugs, but we're the ones who have the drugs!"

I gasped as Tyler opened his leather jacket and showed me several neatly wrapped plastic bags.

He chuckled. "Only you're really selling them for us. Got it now, pretty boy?"

Tyler shoved several packages into my shirt. I tried to knock them away, but checked myself when I spotted Mr. Simpson roaming the halls and stopping to chat with several groups of students. Just then the bell for class sounded. I quickly closed my shirt to cover the stash and stood boldly by my sister while the White Boys scurried in the opposite direction of Mr. Simpson.

The principal and I exchanged quick glances. Then Jennifer and I hustled to our next classes. Unknown to the White Boys, I didn't fear exposure to Mr. Simpson. Constable Howard had included him in our plans with the White Boys, and he'd reluctantly agreed to turn a blind eye during supposed drug exchanges. The constable assured Mr. Simpson that the drugs were harmless substitutes, and that drug trafficking in his school was just a setup to stop the real thing from happening.

"You okay, Stilts?" I asked, using her hated nickname to distract her from the situation.

"No, I'm not!" she snapped. "And stop using that wretched name."

"Sorry, Jen!"

We walked silently down the hall. I steered Jennifer past her 10:00 a.m. history class, down the back stairs, and into the school cafeteria. I bought each of us some hot chocolate, which we drank at a small window table in the far corner.

"What are we going to do with those drugs?" Jennifer whispered.

I looked around the cafeteria and saw that it was mostly empty. Three other students sat a table on the other side of the room, doing the same thing Jennifer and I were doing. Just talking. The custodian nodded a quiet hello as he pushed his broom between the tables. We stood and pushed other chairs back for him. He smiled his thanks and moved down the aisle, whistling softly to himself.

"The drugs, Jason! What are we going to do with the drugs?"

"I'll give them to Andrew. He'll then give me the money we were supposed to get from the sales. Then I'll give the cash to Tyler."

"But Tyler will know if the drugs aren't delivered," Jennifer said.

"Not really. I'm meeting him again on Friday after school to give him the money. We all meet at the Cedar Swamp Schoolhouse on Saturday night. That doesn't leave much time for any of Tyler's customers to complain to him. It's a risk we'll have to take."

"What about the money? How will Constable Howard get it back?"

"All the bills are marked," I said. "They can be easily traced if any of the boys try to use them."

I looked deeply into Jennifer's eyes and saw the fear. I, too, trembled as I reached across to clasp her hand. I wanted to say everything would be all right, but I knew that too many things could easily go wrong. I just knew I completely trusted Constable Howard and Andrew. Mom and Dad had faith in me to protect Jennifer. That was what kept me going. It had to!

Chapter 13

The following Saturday was the first weekend of the March break. The weather gave us a good beginning to the holiday. Warm temperatures, clear skies, and lots of sunshine melted the winter snow. Patches of green lawn peeked through the last layers. Highways and roads were bare and dry to slightly muddy along the country lanes.

I sat nervously at the kitchen table, wishing the night was over. I missed the museum. The thirty hours of community service that seemed so humiliating a month ago had actually been fun. I had learned more about the history of the Donnellys and had taken a greater interest in Granddad's study of ghosts. Even meeting Finnegan seemed better than waiting for the midnight hour.

"Any last questions, Jason? Jennifer?" Constable Howard asked.

He'd spent the evening with us going over last-minute plans. Andrew didn't join us at the house. At this moment he was at the museum archives researching a local history project due after the holiday. He still needed to keep his cover as a local teen high school student. Before I could answer, Mom jumped in. "Tom, you're sure the kids will be safe?"

"Ellen, I know you're frightened," Dad said. "So are we all. But this has to be done."

"I know," Mom said quietly, "but …"

Constable Howard jumped into the conversation. "Let's go over the plan again."

We all breathed easier as Mom settled in her chair to listen.

"Tom drops the kids off at the museum," Constable Howard began. "Andrew will quickly jump into the back of the car as he exits with the day's crowd. I've planted some of my other constables and their families in the museum to act as visitors to distract from Andrew's exit at closing time. Your grandfather will be there, too, just to make it look as normal as possible. I'll also cruise by to attract the attention of any unwanted spies. Andrew will then wait with you and Ellen.

"At 11:00 p.m. he'll use your car to pick up Jennifer and Jason at the museum. If anyone sees the family car at the museum at that time, they won't be suspicious. From there the three of them will head out to Cedar Swamp Schoolhouse. The White Boys should already be there, and the Boss will follow closer to midnight. The drug squad will be in our spotter van parked three lanes down the road. The farmer agreed to let us leave it there with a FOR SALE sign on it for the past three days. Andrew's also wearing a remote microphone and will let us know when the Boss arrives.

"Andrew then waits until the drugs and money exchange hands with the Boss before giving the signal to the squad outside. We rush in and make the arrests. At no time will Jason or Jennifer be in any real danger. The Boss isn't known to carry any guns and, in fact, prefers to avoid firearms."

"Some comfort!" Mom whispered.

Constable Howard ignored her comment and tried his best to be patient. "I think it's time, Jason."

We both left the table, but not without hugging Mom first. She clung for several moments to Jennifer's hand until Dad reached over and pried her fingers away. He stayed close to her as we left the kitchen.

Here, Jason!" he called. "Start the car. I'll be there in a minute."

"Cold?" I asked Jennifer lamely as we started down the stairs.

"No!" she insisted.

I opened the passenger door for her and scraped the thick frost from the window. I did the same for all the other windows, and when I climbed into the car, *I* was cold. My frosty breath clouded the inside of the window again. I fumbled with the keys in my numb fingers as I tried to insert the right one in the ignition. I dropped them between the pedals.

"Gloves would help!" Jennifer suggested.

I let the remark go. Finding the key, I finally put it in the ignition and turned. The engine groaned slowly. Releasing the turn, I waited a few moments. I pumped the gas three times the way Dad had told me, held down the gas pedal, and tried the ignition again. The engine groaned, but then turned into a continuous roar. The whole car shuddered. I let go of the starter, and the car stalled. I pounded my fists on the steering wheel. Jennifer reached over and grabbed my hands.

There was no smart remark, just a gentle squeeze. I relaxed again.

"It's flooded, Jason. No point in trying again. Let it rest. Dad said the extra gas would drain from the carburetor in a minute."

I cranked the engine one more time, and it caught just as Dad opened the driver's door. I jumped out to make room for him and slid into the back passenger seat.

"Start okay?" he asked.

"A little sluggish," I admitted.

"Time for a tune-up, I guess," he said.

The rest of the drive passed silently. As we drove up to

the front door of the museum, the last of the crowd was just exiting. Dad braked quickly as two kids darted out in front of the car. He waved his apologies at the young parents who had each of their squirming children firmly in a hand grip. Jennifer and I got out of the car, and Andrew hustled down the steps and through the rear passenger door I'd left open. I started to close the door when I saw the Caddie idling in the street at the end of the alley.

"Dad, look!" I whispered. "It's the Caddie. The Boss is here."

"Mr. Stevens, don't look!" Andrew ordered. "Jason, I saw him, too. He pulled in just as I got into the car. It isn't likely he saw me. Just turn and walk into the museum. Your grandfather's waiting like he always is. Good luck. I'll see you later." He reached over and tapped Dad on the shoulder, and my father drove away.

Just before Jennifer and I entered the museum, I glanced down the alley. Constable Howard's OPP cruiser blocked my view of the main street. The intersection cleared, and the Caddie disappeared.

I sighed. "He left!"

"What? Who?" Jennifer mumbled.

"The Caddie! The Boss! They're both gone!"

Smiling at Granddad, I shut the front door, flipped the CLOSED sign over, and walked to the back room. For the next few hours Jennifer and I mopped floors, cleaned bathrooms, and dusted display cases. Granddad worked in the curator's office, organizing files for the archives. I heard the grandfather clock in the front foyer strike eleven times.

"Eleven already?" Jennifer asked.

"Andrew will be here any minute."

Jennifer's pale face twitched. She nervously brushed her

drooping hair and fumbled with her gold necklace.

"You okay?" I asked.

"Just a little chilly, that's all."

"Yeah, you're right. Let me check the thermostat. Granddad turns down the heat every night. It helps protect some of the artifacts that aren't in display cases."

I picked up the mops and pail of dirty water to take them to the back room. Using my rear end to push the door bar, I stumbled into the back room, slopped water from the pail, and slid on the wet floor.

"Dumb, Jason! Really dumb!" I muttered to myself as I set the pail down.

I dropped one of the mops and began to clean up my mess. Then I noticed the temperature starting to get colder. The air grew moister, and I could see my breath mist. I looked over my shoulder to check the back door. Then I saw it!

"Jen! Grandpa!" I called. "Come quick! I think Finnegan's back."

I pointed at the back wall of the storeroom. All three of us watched the faint, round light grow larger and brighter.

"There's a message," Granddad said as he adjusted his glasses. We stepped closer and squinted through the glare where the message flickered: STOP THEM!

"Stop who?" Jennifer wondered.

Granddad and I didn't answer immediately.

"Could he mean the White Boys and the Boss?" I suggested. "We're meeting them later tonight at the Cedar Swamp Schoolhouse. The White Boys have threatened to raid the Saltses' farm. It's the old Donnelly homestead. Maybe Finnegan's trying to tell us something about that."

"Who else could it be?" Granddad asked. "I wish I was going with you."

"Granddad, not —" Jennifer said, but she didn't finish. We all jumped at the sudden blast of a car horn. "What's that?" she asked.

"It can't be Andrew," I said. "He's supposed to come to the back door. Go see, Jen."

Jennifer scowled at the abrupt order I'd given. "It's the taxi that Grandma sent for you, Granddad."

"That woman," he growled. "Always spoiling my fun."

Jennifer came to the storeroom with Granddad's winter clothes and boots. He grumbled as she helped him dress. "There, Granddad," she said as she tied his scarf neatly under his chin. "Here's your hat. Pull the ear flaps down. It's cold out there."

"I should be going with you. Take care of them, Finnegan, wherever you are," Granddad said as he headed toward the front of the museum and the taxi outside.

"Have a safe trip home, Granddad," Jennifer said. "And take your special medicine when you get home."

"Medicine! What special medicine?" With a twinkle in his eye he tipped his cap with two fingers and left the museum.

We both laughed, then jumped at the taps on the back door.

"Andrew!" I said, rushing to the back door.

"Jason, look," Jennifer said.

I stared at the wall. The written message started to blur, and the light faded, then disappeared.

Jennifer frowned. "Finnegan's gone."

"I guess he got his message across as best he could." I said, opening the door to let Andrew in.

"Message?" Andrew asked. "What message?"

Jennifer giggled. "Nothing you're interested in."

"Besides, we're ready to go," I added.

We hustled into the idling car. Andrew drove cautiously to the main street and lingered to check for any parked cars. We saw the cruiser parked at Tim Hortons.

"It's not like Constable Howard to frequent that place while on duty," I muttered.

"Only adding to the cover," Andrew said. "If the Boss is following us or plans to surprise us, he'll think Doug is too busy filling his face with doughnuts and coffee."

We said nothing more as we crossed the old railway bed and headed south of town. Passing the Roman Line and the brightly lit St. Patrick's Church, Andrew made a left turn on Highway 7 at Elginfield, then turned again on Highway 23 north.

"The old Cedar Swamp Road," he muttered to no one in particular. "Cedar Swamp School next stop."

Jennifer gripped my arm more tightly as we parked on the side road that paralleled the schoolhouse. We all climbed out of the car and looked around the property anxiously. In the melting mounds of snow, I saw fresh prints leading to the back door of the schoolhouse.

"Fools!" Andrew sneered. He pointed at the faint glow reflected in the rectangular school window.

"They've lit a fire, which can be seen for miles. Just what we need — to have a neighbour phone in with another complaint."

Andrew followed the previous footsteps one at a time so as not to create any more fresh tracks in the snow. We did the same and arrived at the back door puffing heavily. Without knocking, Andrew pushed the door open. "Nice going, you idiots!" he shouted.

The White Boys jumped, and we heard a clatter of glass at Tyler's feet.

"No wonder you're not thinking right. You're all drunk again." Andrew held up a small, almost-empty bottle of rye whiskey.

"It's cold in here," Tyler whined as he grabbed the bottle from Andrew.

"One of you idiots douse that fire!" Andrew ordered. "And hide that bottle. If the Boss sees either one, the deal's off. Then we're all in trouble."

"Stevens, do as he says!" Tyler barked. He took one last swig from the bottle before hiding it in an inside pocket.

I quickly scuffed some frozen dirt over the burning coals. Jennifer threw some handfuls of snow that had drifted in small mounds under the window frames and door jambs. She stayed close to me. Finally, only choking wisps of black smoke floated throughout the large schoolroom.

The other White Boys sat on an old riding lawn mower, twisted lawn furniture, and wooden school benches. Andrew and Tyler stood for the longest time trying to out-stare each other. Tyler didn't like being ordered around by Andrew. I could see the anger building in his tightened face.

"Hey, Tyler," one of the White Boys called, "where's that bottle? I need warming up."

"Not now!" Andrew snapped.

Tyler stepped in to jostle Andrew. "I give the orders to my boys, Smith."

Andrew just ignored him, then cried, "Headlights! Get down!"

We all crawled below the windows. Andrew and I peered over the lower ledge and saw three short blinks of bright lights — it was the Caddie!

"It's the Boss!" Andrew quickly answered with three blinks from his flashlight.

The Caddie's interior light flipped on as the Boss, followed by J.T., left the car. The two drug peddlers walked clumsily toward the schoolhouse, ignoring their footprints in the snow. They didn't even bother to knock but barged into the schoolhouse, which was lit only by Andrew's lone flashlight.

"Taking a chance someone will see you, Boss?" Andrew asked.

The Boss cackled. "Out here in this desolate cold? Not a chance. Besides, Howard's hunkered down at the doughnut shop in town. He won't be coming out this way. Let's get this done."

He flipped open his camel-hair overcoat and pulled out two large square shapes wrapped neatly in green plastic wrap. "This is it! The best money can buy."

As Tyler moved quickly to grab the bags, he stopped and raised his hand to his face. "What's that?"

A bright pinprick of light from the window caught his eye, and he held up his hands to block it.

"I don't see anything," Andrew growled.

"There's a light in the window over there!" Tyler yelled. "Someone's out there!"

Andrew raced over to the window. The light, if there had been any at all, was gone. He stayed for the longest time. I joined him, and Jennifer followed. He nodded down the moonlit road. We all saw the shadow of a van sneaking along the highway. Its lights were out.

"Nothing there," Andrew said. "It might have been the reflection of my flashlight in the window. Sorry."

Tyler and the Boss stared at Andrew for several seconds, not sure what to think of his explanation.

"Who's this character now?" Tyler snarled.

"Enough!" the Boss ordered. "J.T., watch the road from that window. Where's the money, Smith?"

Andrew fumbled in his coat to take out a wad of paper bills. Again I saw the flash of light in the opposite side window of the school. I knew it wasn't Andrew's flashlight.

"Finnegan!" Jennifer whispered. She had seen it, too!

Chapter 14

Andrew and the Boss exchanged drugs and money. The Boss counted the bills one by one, while Tyler greedily tore away the green plastic covering on one of the drug packages. Slowly unfolding it, he picked some strands and placed them in a cigarette paper, then rolled and lit it. He dragged deeply, and a smile crept across his face.

"Hey, that's our stuff, too!" one of the other White Boys snapped as he lurched toward Tyler.

"Not so fast!" Tyler ordered, pushing him away. But then he stopped and all the blood rushed out of his face. "There it is again!"

This time everyone looked. The glob of light grew bigger and brighter. Jennifer reached for me. We saw Tyler and the other White Boys cower and heard faint whimpers as the light started to take form.

"Jason," Jennifer whispered, "it really is Finnegan."

I held her more tightly.

"What is this?" the Boss demanded, rallying from his own shock. He fumbled with his money, and some of the bills slipped to the dirt floor. A cool draft of air blew them closer to the still-smouldering fire, yet he didn't try to retrieve them. Finnegan reached his full form and walked toward the old slate board at the front of the schoolhouse. Lifting his arm, he wrote in bold letters: MURDER! STOP THEM!

Tyler bolted in panic. As he passed Jennifer and me, she

stuck out her foot to trip him. Tyler did a looping dive into the firepit and screamed. He lay still, trying to recover his breath, then let out another scream. His jacket had caught fire. The other White Boys grabbed the discarded drug package and raced to the door. They collided with the drug squad coming from the outside.

"Freeze!" Constable Howard shouted.

The Boss feebly stuffed the money into an inside pocket, but Constable Howard grabbed his wrist. He twisted it to force the Boss to loosen his grip. Andrew meanwhile pinned J.T. and cuffed his hands behind his back.

"You're all under arrest!" Constable Howard said.

"What for?" Tyler demanded. "You got nothing on me. I got no drugs. Look to them other guys."

"But I saw you light up," Andrew said. "And, Boss, the bills you have are marked, so we can prove they came from tonight."

"Who are you, anyway?" the Boss asked. "You always did seem too smart to be one of these stupid jerks."

"My real name's Andrew Smith, but I'm with Special Operations of the OPP, assigned to the drug squad. I've been watching you for the past six months, hoping to get a chance like this."

"You'll pay for this, Smith." J.T. growled, struggling to free himself.

Andrew pushed him over to two other constables, who dragged him away. "You'll be paying first, J.T. About five to seven years, I'd say."

The Boss knew it was over. His rights read, he said nothing that could be used against him by the law. He offered no struggle as the officers led him away.

Constable Howard, Jennifer, Andrew, and I stood in the

dimly lit schoolhouse.

"Look, Jason," Jennifer said.

We had forgotten Finnegan. Through the scuffling, he'd stayed near the chalkboard ledge. His message started to fade. His own light grew dimmer. He raised a hand in a small wave, and a soft whisper came from his mouth. *"Thank you."*

"You're welcome!" Jennifer said.

"And thank you!" I added.

Finnegan then turned and walked slowly toward the door, fading with each step he took. He disappeared before he reached the outside.

"What was that?" Andrew gasped.

Constable Howard chuckled. He had heard the many stories from Granddad about the spiritual world. "That's a forerunner," he explained to Andrew. "We think he may have been a part of the Donnelly tragedy many years ago. According to Jason's grandfather, he became trapped between the physical world and the spiritual world. He was destined to stay there until he repaid a wrong he might have done that night on February 4, 1880."

"You're kidding, aren't you?" The smirk on Andrew's face faded when Constable Howard shook his head.

"Think about it, Andrew. We knew the White Boys planned another raid on the Salts farm. Mr. Stevens nearly lost his life when they raided his place and burnt his barn. Maybe Finnegan didn't want to see the violence around here grow to what it had been in his day. He's paying for his mistakes by warning us."

"Will he come back?" Andrew asked.

"I don't know," I said. "Granddad would probably say no. Finnegan's completed his task and paid his debt. I imagine he'll now be able to cross over to the spiritual world and be at peace."

"Wow!" Andrew murmured. "You just never know."

We all laughed and patted Andrew on the shoulder, while Jennifer shyly hugged him.

"Let's go home, folks!" Constable Howard said. "It's been a long day, and the Stevenses will be worried about their kids."

Epilogue

Jennifer and I followed all the newspaper stories and police reports leading up to the trial. The Boss and J.T. appeared in court where the judge remanded them for trial in May on bail of ten thousand dollars each. The Boss paid and hired himself an expensive Toronto lawyer to defend him. J.T., unable to pay the bail, stayed in jail. Feeling betrayed, he testified against the Boss in return for a reduced sentence. Tyler and the White Boys accepted similar offers. Lucan returned to being a sleepy village.

Now we all sat in the warm spring sunshine of a mid-May afternoon. Constable Howard bleeped his siren as he turned into our driveway.

Mom rose from her chair on the porch and waved. "Doug," she called, "join us for some lemonade. We're celebrating summer early."

"Don't mind if I do," he said. "Shift's just about over. I have one more job to do before the end of the day." He climbed the steps, but before sitting down between Dad and Granddad, he handed me a letter.

"For me?" I saw the address of the London courthouse on the envelope.

"It's your official release from probation, Jason," the constable said.

My hands shook as I opened the letter and silently read the message. Another page dropped from my hands, and

Dad stooped to pick it up. Looking up from my letter, I saw both Dad and Granddad smile.

"What is it?" Jennifer asked as she and Mom returned with a fresh pitcher of lemonade. Dad handed the sheet to them.

"Oh, Jason!" Mom started to cry.

I held my breath, waiting for the bad news to come. Had I been charged with drug trafficking? But Constable Howard had said he'd put in a good word for me at the probation board.

Jennifer took the certificate and handed it to me. "It's a citizen's commendation for promoting public safety in the community of Lucan."

"I don't understand. I should be going to jail."

"After your hearing with the probation board," Constable Howard explained, "I told them I had you under surveillance the whole of your community service. You were really providing me with information to stop the drug trafficking in the Lucan area. Along with Andrew's confirmation, we succeeded in discrediting the testimony of the White Boys and J.T., who claimed that you and Jennifer were both involved with drugs."

Mom reached over and gave Constable Howard a huge hug, then kissed him on the cheek. Granddad reached over and warmly shook his hand. Grandma cried.

"Hi, Mr. Stevens!" A paper thudded at our feet on the porch.

Dad laughed. "Nice toss, Jimmy!"

"Who was that?" I asked.

"Jimmy Parks, a new delivery boy for the Lucan newspaper," Dad said as he unfolded the paper. "Hey, Dad! Mom! You're front-page news. Quite a day for the Stevens family."

We all gathered around Dad's chair. There, on the front

page, was a picture of Granddad, Grandma, and Mayor Tom McLaughlin holding a ribbon. Granddad was using a large pair of silver scissors to cut it.

Jennifer pointed at the headline: LOCAL HISTORIAN OPENS NEW MUSEUM WING. "It's your article, Dad."

"I interviewed the mayor shortly after the opening," Dad said. "He had some interesting things to say about the Donnellys and their place in Lucan's history."

"Like what?" I asked.

"Here," Dad said, "I'll read you his quote about the Donnelly murders. He gave it to a reporter in the *Toronto Star*: 'It was a black mark on the community. They murdered a whole family. That's not too good, is it?' He really hopes to create a Donnelly display in the museum and give recognition to the terrible deed done to the family."

"What's his stake in this?" Jennifer asked. "Why the sudden change? I thought everyone here wanted the whole story hushed up."

"Well, things change, Jennifer," Dad said. "For one thing, I found out that the mayor is the great-great-great-nephew of Martin McLaughlin, a resident in Lucan at the time of the Donnellys. His Uncle Martin belonged to the 'society' from St. Patrick's Parish that wanted to stop the thieving in the community. Members of the drunken mob that raided the Donnelly farm that night in 1880 also belonged to that society. Mr. McLaughlin grew up on the Roman Line and remembers his father's embarrassment about the crimes. More people are starting to think the same way."

"You bet!" Granddad interrupted. "And about time, too! Lots of people laugh at Rob Salts and his ghost stories about the old Donnelly homestead, but he knows more about the true story of that family than anyone I know. He's getting more and more people touring his property. He even told me that a descendant of Grouchy Ryder, one of the Donnellys' best friends of the time, came to visit. His business is going great."

"That's another reason," Dad continued. "A lot of tourist business opportunities will come out of this. The historical society is even planning bus tours to raise money for a future museum expansion. We might even persuade Mr. Lord to give us the original Donnelly tombstone."

I was hooked. "Granddad, could I still work on Saturdays and help you out at the museum?"

"Me, too!" Jennifer demanded.

"I don't know, Stilts," I teased. "You any good at cleaning toilet bowls?" I dodged a crumpled napkin that Jennifer threw my way, and we all laughed.

"Glad to have you both," Granddad said, beaming. He reached over and held Grandma's hand. She smiled warmly at both of us.

"Hi, folks!" We all turned to see Andrew Smith standing at the end of the walk. He no longer wore a black leather jacket. Gone were the black boots with the white laces, and the package of cigarettes bulging from his chest pocket. A new, trimmer haircut had replaced the slicked-back greasy curls that had once fallen over his eyes. "Just wanted to stop by to say hello."

"Andrew!" Jennifer squeaked. She jumped from her chair and bumped the small deck table that held the lemonade pitcher. I reached for the wobbling jug, but the sticky liquid flew in all directions, soaking both Jennifer and me. Jennifer turned an embarrassed scarlet amid the howling laughter.

"Way to go, Stilts!" I said, but I knew she hadn't heard me. She was too busy staring at Andrew as he shyly walked up the steps of our front porch.

A Note from the Author

Although this story is fictional, the references to southwestern Ontario's Donnelly family and the horrible events that occurred on February 4, 1880, are rooted in actual history. Stories about the Donnellys have been a significant part of my life. Besides the many tales my parents told me from the 1940s to the 1960s, my brother, Borden, has reminded me that many of these stories were also shared with hitchhiking Royal Canadian Air Force men returning to their base at Clinton, Ontario, after a weekend leave. At times these airmen would be so enthralled with the Donnelly stories that my father would make a side trip to visit the Donnellys' tombstone (the original) at St. Patrick's Church in Lucan or take a short drive up the Roman Line to see the original homestead.

I reacquainted myself with the Donnelly family in the late 1960s and early 1970s by reading popular accounts of the family by Thomas P. Kelley (*The Black Donnellys*, *Vengeance of the Donnellys*) and Orlo Miller (*The Donnellys Must Die* and *Death to the Donnellys*). In the 1970s, noted playwright and poet James Reaney published and had produced his masterful trilogy of plays, *Sticks and Stones*, *The St. Nicholas Hotel*, and *Handcuffs*, known collectively as *The Donnellys*. During the 1990s, more scholarly historical publications on the Donnellys began to appear such as Ray Fazakas's *The Donnelly Album*, which thoroughly depicts in words and pictures the Donnellys' life in the Lucan area in the nineteenth century.

During the years that Molly, my wife, and I drove our daughter, Beth, past the intersection of Highways 7 and 23 (the old Cedar Swamp Road), through Elginfield and Birr to the University of Western Ontario's Huron College, I discovered a copy of J. Robert Salts's book *You Are Never Alone: Our Life on the Donnelly Homestead* at the local general store in Birr.

After reading his book, I arranged for a tour of the Donnelly Homestead with Mr. Salts. It was a very entertaining day (July 26, 2000, my fifty-second birthday) that Molly and I spent with Mr. Salts under the chestnut trees dedicated by William Donnelly himself in memory of his family and the terrible events that occurred on that night when five of his kin were murdered. I walked away impressed, as well as pleasantly entertained, with Mr. Salts's life at the Donnelly Homestead and his detailed research on the Donnelly family's tragic fate.

Selected Reading

Boyle, Terry. *Haunted Ontario*. Toronto: Polar Express, 1998.

Colley, Peter. *The Donnellys: A Drama with Music*. Toronto: Simon & Pierre/The Dundurn Group, 1974.

Colombo, John Robert. *Ghost Stories of Canada*. Toronto: The Dundurn Group, 2000.

____. *Ghost Stories of Ontario*. Toronto: The Dundurn Group, 1996.

Edwards, Peter. *Night Justice: The True Story of the Black Donnellys*. Toronto: Key Porter Books, 2005.

____. "Town of Lucan Wants to Banish Shame of Murders," *Toronto Star*, February 6, 2005.

Fazakas, Ray. *The Donnelly Album*. Willowdale, ON: Firefly Books, 1995.

Feltes, Norman N. *This Side of Heaven: Determining the Donnelly Murders, 1880*. Toronto: University of Toronto Press, 1999.

Geringer, Joseph. *The Black Donnellys: Canada's Tragic Roustabouts*. *www.crimelibrary.com*: Courtroom Television Network LLC, 2003.

Kelley, Thomas P. *The Black Donnellys*. Willowdale, ON: Firefly Books, 1993.

____. *Vengeance of the Black Donnellys*. Willowdale, ON: Firefly Books, 1995.

Miller, Orlo. *Death to the Donnellys*. Toronto: Signet, 1979.

____. *The Donnellys Must Die*. Mississauga, ON: John Wiley and Sons Canada, 2006.

Official Donnelly Home Page: *www.donnellys.com*.

Reaney, James. *The Donnellys (Sticks and Stones, The St. Nicholas Hotel, Handcuffs).* Toronto: The Dundurn Group, 2008.

Ryder, Earl. "The Truth About the Donnelly Massacre." *earl@netcom.ca*: Earl Ryder, 1999.

Salts, J. Robert. *You Are Never Alone: Our Life on the Donnelly Homestead.* London, ON: J. Robert Salts, 1996.

Smith, Barbara. *Ontario Ghost Stories.* Edmonton: Lone Pine Publishing, 1998.